An Awful Lot Like Me

An Awful Lot Like Me

A Novella

David Stoeckl

ISBN – 979-8-230977-21-6 – ebook
ISBN - 978-1-967695-02-7 – Printed Book

For further information, contact Albedo Books at: albedobooks@gmail.com

An Awful Lot Like Me

Have you ever sat at the bus stop just to watch the people go by? Now I don't mean while you're waiting for the bus. I mean, like, you have nowhere you have to be while everyone else does. You can watch while hanging out on some street corner or in the mall. I don't think it matters. Mostly, I like it because it's friendly, but you don't have to get involved.

So you see, I just got paid, and the more I think about what I wanna buy, the more restless I get and the more restless I get, the more I walk around and the more I walk around, the more I wanna move on. But, I didn't see it at first. Then one night, I was at this coffee house, resting on a bench, reading the graffiti carved into the table, and I thought, "This table's just a wall with legs. Y'know? And like, here I am, cup in hand, facing a wall that goes nowhere." That's when I realized that I had to get out of here.

So, look at me now. Parked I some café in downtown Sacramento waiting for my bus to leave; wondering if I shouldn't've regretted my decision. It makes me feel kind of down &, , , y'know ------ ti r

e

d

.

My head rests beside my cup as I close my eyes, ready to accept any reason to not live.

"May I sit with you?"

Startled, I sat up suddenly. A tall, most unappealing figure takes the seat beside me. Suspiciously, I examine the intruder. Middle-ages or so, thin mustache, dark eyes, dark hair and a very dark complexion. A dimple bores its way into each cheek. I notice a huge knife in its sheath, attached to his belt, and decide he's not someone I really want to get to know. I'm just about to get up to move to another table, but realize that would be rude. At least he had the courtesy to ask before seating himself.

"May I buy you a cup of coffee?" he offers.

Shifting in my seat, I hold up my half-filled cup and wonder what he wants. I know he wants something.

The stranger smiles, but his smile is more leering than attractive, with a big, gold front tooth that appears to be tarnished or decayed.

"Aquino is my Christian name," he boasts, holding out a hand. His deep voice is broad and commanding. My table just became his table. I accept his handshake cautiously, then I hear the man announce our time to reboard. Hastily, I excuse myself and revive my senses as I climb onto the coach. Reclaiming my seat, I reach into my pack and pull out a book. Then, I see the stranger, Aquino approach along the narrow corridor. He winks at me as he passes, his smile still covering his face. As I look back at him through the space between the seats, I see a bright, red bandana trailing out of his denim pocket.

As our caravan heads out, I turn to my novel, but I hear Aquino in the back with who I suppose is his family. They are laughing and singing different songs. I glance back and see this bigger-than-life knife leave its sheath. It slices through a mold of salami and one of cheese in two quick flashes, silent as rain before it touches the ground.

Our bus continues to chug-up through the Sierra Nevadas. I watch the dusk darken my world so, worn by the day, I try to sleep, but the seats are uncomfortable and I can't relax. I hear Aquino's voice throughout the bus. His laughter fills the gloom with its engraved mockery. I shift around in my seat. They're too hard to get comfortable. Through the space between the seats, I watch them. He sits beside a woman I guess to be his wife. She laughs at everything he says while she brushes her long, dark hair. I can see there are two others seated in front of them, but I can't see them as easily as Aquino.

I switch on the overhead light and try to read again. The watered-down plot eventually lulls me into a restless sleep. Then, something arouses me. I awaken to find Aquino, sitting next to me.

"You did not sleep well, my friend," he grunts.

I try to clear my head while groping for any answer. His features seem distorted when he grins, yet somehow his smile is almost angelic behind his discoloured teeth.

"Where do you travel to, boy?"

I clear a particle out of my eye before answering. "Uh, Reno, to work, before I head East. I heard that anyone can get a job in Reno doing something."

"How'd you like to work for me for a short while? I do not pay much. I'd like some help on a menial job. I'm becoming an old man now and a younger shoulder would lighten my load."

"How much?" I ask, ready to set priorities.

He smiles again. "I can provide you a place to sleep and warm food to eat. When the job is complete, your ticket shall be provided and probably some money, depending on how long you stay. What do you say, boy?"

"What kind of work?"

"Our old truck needs some repairs on the engine and if you remain long enough, her camper is long overdue for a facelift."

"I'm no mechanic," I admit.

He shrugs it off as though it is of no concern.

I lean against the cold window as the lights of Reno come into sight. Coming up from the warmer Sacramento sunshine, I don't look forward to the chilly nights. The frosty window against my cheek suggests I should stay with this unorthodox group. I turn to Aquino, still sitting beside me, and nod.

He smiles.

His wages are delivered as stated. A warm place to stay, (if you don't mind a tent with a fire), and lots of tasty, warm food to eat.

There are two members of his "household" that I seldom see, even with the closeness of our lifestyles and living conditions. One is Aquino's teenaged daughter, Rachel, whose braided hair is almost as long as her mother's. The other is their twelve year old son, Michal. He would speak to me when I least expected it, though never more than three words in a sentence. I seldom saw either of them, never saw them together and always thought about them.

It's a cold morning. The window shutter I'm repairing won't stay in place. The more I work, the less it cooperates. Aquino is on the other side of the truck doing who cares what. It must be a tragic comedy for him to listen to me, between my efforts and speaking my mind to a window shutter.

"Come on, baby. Into place now. That's the way. Oops! No, just hang on until the screw starts. That's it. That's it . . . yeah, that's it. DAMN! DAMN! DAMN IT!" I scream as the blind claims victory again.

Even when I try to pick it up and throw it across the field, the beast leaves a sliver lanced through my finger. I release a moan as blood begins to escape and I hold the wound to my mouth.

Then I see Aquino, laughing, enjoying my humiliation. I start to tell him where he can stick his shutter, but he unexpectedly grabs hold of my arm and swings me around the grounds. His strength surprises me. I orbit until he lets go, and I fight to catch myself. I won't let myself fall.

Again, he laughs his grinding laugh, then suggests, "Go into the camper and have my wife remove that wood." He winks and heads out to retrieve the shutter. As I turn to go, I stumble over my tools, further damaging my pride before I enter the camper.

Mrs. Aquino's not there, although I quickly sense somebody else is. My eyes try to adjust to the low light, and I soon see that it's Rachel, their daughter, doing needlework. A warm smile comes to her face to greet me.

"I, uh, came in, uh, to have a sliver removed...."

"... I know. I heard you outside."

I lean an arm against a cupboard and smile, generally embarrassed. "Yeah, well, uh, I wanted to get this, uh, sliver out, but I see Mrs. A. ain't here."

Her plain, pleasant features return my nervous smile, and she offers, "I can remove a splinter."

"Oh, no thank you," I decline, not wanting to be a bother and she must be busy, and I really am needed back outside plus other acclamations of false modesty and the like and she already has a needle out of her sewing work, heating up the end with a match. I sit down and she singles out the finger, squeezes it beet red, then with two pricks and a pull and the pain is gone. Her

9

concentration eases and her shy smile returns. I thank her a few times, then rise to leave.

"Do you have to go already?" she asks. Her face glows from her seat next to the window.

"I'm sure your papa wants me out there," I respond, still half out of my seat.

She laughs lightly. "You act like he has you on a timeclock. What is he going to do, dock you pay?"

I smile sheepishly and begin to sit back down when suddenly Aquino bellows, "BOY!" and I jump up, almost pulling the table off its stand. A few hanging pans are knocked about as I scurry towards the door. Then, I stop long enough to look back at Rachel to thank her again before opening the door. She chuckles lightly, but her eyes look sad, perhaps woebegone. That face follows me as I step from the van.

Aquino, head under the hood of the truck, motions for me to come. "Come on, boy," he orders when my pace doesn't suit him. I stop beside the truck until he looks out. He's about to speak when I announce, "I am not a dog."

"Then I won't treat you like one," he acknowledges. "Come here and tell me what you think." His smile returns to his face as I lean in.

A few days later we have the engine working like a purr, the camper is pretty much the way Aquino says he likes it and it's our drinking night in town. I sip while Aquino consumes incredible amounts of alcohol, though it doesn't seem to affect him. He stalks through the casino from person to person, selling anything from the ring on his finger to the rims off the truck; sometimes trading, sometimes exchanging addresses for later propositions or deals of offering services. He works through the maze of people, always learning about the various drinkers and gamblers from other patrons. He comes by me, sits down, orders another drink and smiles his crude smile.

"Do you like your night out, boy?"

I nod and take another sip of my drink.

He glances around the room. "How do you like the girls here?"

I shrug. "They're alright, I guess." I'd been studying one waitress, dressed to offer more than just beverages, flirting with a gambler who I guessed to be around fifty. She keeps a constant smile on her face and talks with her eyes. He seems to talk with his pocketbook and she like what she hears. I look at my own patched blue jeans and grease-stained shirt and notice an odd feeling of inadequacy.

Aquino is silent, but his silence doesn't bother me. He's one man who speaks louder by his mannerisms than by his words. Soon someone passes by, and he stands, introduces himself and carefully suggests what he can do for this man. Eventually they sat down at a table to talk.

Later, we walk in silence and shiver through the long walk home. Then Aquino starts to sing:

Spell ye might through the fight
Carry hardships on plight

For the life is not old
Just it sometimes too cold...
And at the end of it all, what a sight....

I clear my throat and hum along. I don't know the tune, but it's an easy one to fake. Then he stops suddenly on "sight", which catches me humming a couple notes.

We resume our silence, (except for the chuckle under Aquino's breath), until he says, "How do you like my family, boy?"

"Alright, I guess, y'know. I ain't had much chance to get to know them."

"What did you expect?"

"Maybe I expected everyone'd be sort of closer to the clan, y'know, or more dependent on each other." He nods and places a hand warmly on my shoulder.

We round the corner and approach our campsite. Everyone is surely in bed, so we creep past the fire and greet the dogs, checking us for identification. They return to their places by the smoldering cinders.

Aquino waves a silent "goodnight" and retires to his camper. The kids, I know, are asleep in the trailer and I shuffle to my tent. Before I crawl in, I notice the flickering light of a match onto the lantern from Aquino's camper. The soft glow follows me in. I light my own candle and lay back before undressing. My sleeping bag is still unmade, with bits of sand clinging to its underside. Eventually I extinguish the candle, undress and crawl inside my cold bag. Soon that shivery chill subsides so my tired eyelids may close to sleep.

My dreams review the active day. I thought Aquino wouldn't quit. He kept pushing, relentlessly, with the wear and tear of the labour. Twice I found myself wondering if I shouldn't be moving along, but I committed myself to work the day out and if it got no better, I could leave tomorrow.

Then something awakens me. I set up, eyes and ear probing. The dim light of Aquino's camper is gone and all I can see is the starry illumination peeking in my tent door. Then, I hear someone breathing. My vital signs accelerate as I realize there's someone else in here.

"Who's there?" I demand.

"Rachel." Her wispy voice is barely audible, yet easily recognizable.

"Oh, Rachel. Wo! What're you doing here? You won't believe how much you scared me. I didn't know if I was gonna have to attack or whah?"

"I'm sorry I started you."

"No. No. No. Don't apologize. Really. I'm just glad it's you and not someone else." She is silent and I begin to wonder why she's actually here."

"What are you thinking, Papa?"

'You do now know, my wife? You who has chosen me above all others you might have married cannot tell what speaks from my heart? Why, I'm surprised you could be so blind. I wish to see our daughter find her home where she would be happiest. Hard, though, the way our children are taught today. Makes it a sin for us to find a husband for her. This is the best we can do to make a home for her."

"I know Papa. I worry for her, too. She's not so much the big girl she thinks. Still, she had to pick her man. I do hope this one works out. He is the fourth and she's not so sure, now, our ways will work."

"I know. I know. But it should be more promising than what she wanted to try. If it'd been up to her, she would've propositioned that boy in the café. That would have gotten nothing but a defensive man."

"What do you think of him, Papa?"

"I like him. At least I like him more than the other peasants she's picked. He has character, as he showed with the shutters. He doesn't drink what I think a man should, but that can be taken care of if he stays with us long enough. Today I put him to the test, and he came through. I'm certain he was more than ready to quite twice, so I'll have to be careful how I work him tomorrow. Let him have it easier without making it look like I'm being kind. That should settle his young senses."

"Papa?"

"Yes, Mama."

"I love you, Papa."

"I love you, Mama, although I seldom tell you. It seems that I have let that word drop from my mouth. Time, I imagine. I guess I am not just a young man anymore."

"You are still my man, Papa. We still show our love in the things we do. When I was a younger girl, I didn't understand, and when you'd do into town and forget to say you love words, I'd think our love was failing, but now I see how our life has passed. I can see how you declare your love for me everyday we are alone, or together."

Aquino chooses the silence of a reassuring hug.

"What do you think they are doing now, Papa?"

"If I know that young stallion, he should be shocked at first, and perhaps afraid, but that should be well past and if they have not crawled inside his bag, they shall be rolling together on top."

"That is what you think, Papa?"
"That is what I think, Mama."

(That is what Rachel expected.)

Her unexpected appearance still has me shaking, which surprises me, now that the danger's long past. I fumble for the matches to light a candle, then realize I'm naked underneath this bag. I remind myself she is totally cloaked by the darkness where she sits, barely an arms length away. I must be equally invisible. As I grab my pants, the silence is disturbed by the scratch of a match to the charcoal. Her brown eyes reflect the light and search under the flame for the candle on the dirt floor of my tent.

"Put that out a moment," I command, "and let me get some pants on." My bluntness is outweighed only by my embarrassment. I see a smile trickle toward her cheek before blowing against the flaming wood. It appears darker than before and I immediately pull pants over flesh. The sounds of the snap and zip echo against the walls of my tent and no sooner am I finished when Rachel reignites another match.

She passes the flame to the wick and we smile uneasily at each other in the flickering warmth.

"How's your finger?" she asks, barely whispering, loud as Sunday morning church bells.

"Fine. I hardly noticed it today. Um, what'd you do all day?"

"Mama and I are working on a new quilt, and we cut out squares this morning. Then, I cut potatoes and celery for dinner tonight, then Michal and I cleaned up the camper and played a game of beans."

"Beans?"

"Uh-huh. It probably has another name, but that's what we always called it. You line up twelve red beans and twelve white beans in a certain order, like this," she motions with her hands, "then roll dice trying to capture rows and control the other color. Some people play you can take away and buy back beans, but we don't play like that. Doubles count for double control unless it's double fives, then...." She looks at me smiling at her pale reflection in the light, then down at the example she drew in the dirt. Her slender fingers remove the impressions, and she looks out the tent flap until her embarrassment subsides.

"I'm sorry," she whispers.

"For what?"

"I don't know. Maybe for being embarrassed. I didn't come here to tell you how to play beans."

"Why did you come here?"

"To see that you were alright. I've come to see you every night since you arrived, but you've never awakened – until tonight. During the day, you are so busy with Papa that I can never talk to you."

"That's the truth! I swear, you're not here half the time. I never see you, and never have a chance to talk to you or Michal."

"Did you not have a chance when I removed the splinter from your finger?"

"I'd hardly call that the most opportune time to get to know each other. I was kind of mad at the stupid shutter while you were removing its stinger."

"And it was wonderful listening to you scream at it," she taunts. It was my turn to redirect embarrassment.

"Well, tell me about yourself," I request, changing the subject. "Have you always lived in a camper?"

"Uh-huh. We've had this one since I was a small child."

"Do you have any friends?"

"Just Michal, and sometimes that's not such a blessing. We have family all over the country and we visit them regularly. I enjoy the time with my cousins, but usually I just spend time at home. There's much work to do always and not so much time for myself. My grandfather lived like this, and my great-grandfather lived out of a caravan, drawn by a horse all his life. I'm in good company. Our family is very close."

"Yeah, I guess," I respond, moved. "Well, Michal must know you're here."

"That shadow knows everything that goes on. He know where everybody is all the time."

"Does he say anything?"

"Oh, yes. He teases me every night."

"Well then, he might be right outside the tent right now."

"Oh no. If Papa ever caught him, it'd be the last thing he ever did."

I'm uncertain whether to take her literally and opt not to.

"Does Aquino, your Papa, know you're here?"

"Oh yes. He knows."

"And he approves?"

"Yes," her words come slowly. "He hopes you will have me." She tries to hold her gaze but must look away. She's made the move and now waits to see what I will do.

Her words echo through my mind, and I recall Aquino, casually mentioning Rachel, without husband and moderate inquiries of my future plans, if any. I had imagined Aquino playing matchmaker some evening around the dinner fire. Not this.

Then, chiding myself, I imagine myself in black boots, a white silk shirt loosely hanging around my body, and a silk sash tied around my waist. I'd have a bandana wrapped around my head and a large, gold earing in one ear.

I look at Rachel, sleek and beautiful in the candlelight, a warm wool shawl wrapped around her shoulders, still waiting patiently for my response. I could reach over right now, accept her offer and seal it by inviting her in my sack. Few moments will ever be as sacred as this one right now, but I step lightly. This isn't for the night. This is for a lifetime, becoming a permanent member of Aquino's caravan until time takes him to his rest and I, the Papa and Rachel the Mama, carry on the traditions of the family. Funny, still, it's actually quite the offer when there's little reason to say, "No."

On the other hand, when I consider how well I know Rachel, I can't help but think she's offered to consummate the relationship before it begins.

"Is 'love' included with your offer?" I abruptly ask.

The surprise on her face is apparent. None of the others had ever considered love as a qualification for enlistment into the family. She relaxes enough to smile.

"Love is that something I have always been taught and still have never learned," she admits. "The love I understand is very simple, learned from caring for my family. I think I could love you some day, though there is so much I still do not know. When I discover another type of love that might bring us closer together, then both of us can uncover it so that we may learn together. Still, the time is tonight. Papa wants me to share my bed with you so that you might find me acceptable and take me as your wife. It's your choice. You've seen very little of me, but you've seen what I can do."

I meet her eye-to-golden-brown-eye and realize the temptation is growing. I have this overwhelming desire to agree, bring her close and secure the whole deal, but I must talk this over directly with Aquino and in conclusion, I answer, "No, please, , , ," I stop.

Almost immediately a small tear, reflected in the candlelight, crawls down her cheek, then another and my heart aches to see her sadness.

The, she catches a tear from her cheek and brushes it against mine. I can feel my own blood become diluted in my veins and my eyes become moist with my own tears. She whispers something which sounds like an apology.

"No, wait," I plea. "I haven't decided, really. I just have to think it through a bit; talk to Aquino. Y'know? Please don't think bad of this night. Now listen. As it is, I can't turn you away completely. It would be nice if you stay with me, at least for a while, but then please be gone before the sun begins to rise."

She remains unmoved, so I cup her thin face with the palms of my hands and lead her to my side. I spread out my bag and pull a couple of blankets over us. Soon we are comfortable and warm, and I have to admit the temptation is awful, having her cuddle so close. We talk lightly, then I say goodnight, kiss her forehead and eventually fall asleep. When I awaken, she is gone, and I see the first specks of light seeping in my tent as the dawn arises.

I slip back into sleep, sure that Aquino will soon fetch me for the day's labors. The frosty air tries to crash my slumber party as I burrow down deep into the warmth of my sleeping bag.

Then I sit up. It's mid-morning. Aquino would have been up and the morning fire re-ignited. The morning's work should have been scheduled and well underway, but the total map is redrawn as I set up, look outside my old tent and realize they have left.

I find a small note, tied to the strings of my pack, which reads:

Please forgive us, my son. Time had given us the answer we

awaited, and thus, came our time to move on. I hope that you understand. Me and my family are grateful for your service and hope that you may come to work with us again. The future shall tell us all what we are to do.

I leave you this satchel of food and money to take you on

your way. Again, I thank you from the depths of my soul.

Aquino

Can you believe that? Gone. Capute. Total and complete, like they were never there. No more than a dream. I shiver, shocked and bruised beside the remains of the campfire.

Eventually, though the initial shock evolves, a deeper sense of grief develops as I realize what I had and that it is gone.

I search through the satchel but am not hungry. I pack up my few belongings, hoist my pack upon my shoulders and trek on down the road. My senses cool, as I knew they would, while my mind considers my next plan of action.

I pack out to the Big Road, Interstate 80, stretching out before me like a ribbon, held by many asphalt bows and ribbons, wrapping the gift to all, Earth.

The aroma of diesel fuel and oily rubber invites me along. I stick out my thumb to move on, yet a sad, remorseful smile shadows my face. Every person driving past looks like Aquino, or his wife, or Rachel or Michal. Every passing car makes its convoy alone. Kind of like me.

An awful lot like me.

An Awful Lot Like Her

2 Years Later

The fragmented sunshine strives to warm the Earth. I soak in the welcome warmth until high stratus clouds hide its face. A light breeze drifts over these flatlands and I pull my jacket up close around my neck.

It's been an idle, barely productive afternoon on the roof of this three-story warehouse. I glance at my watch, praying for the shift to end. Days like today never passed quickly enough. Still gazing at the dial of my cheap, digital watch, I hear footsteps approach on the gravel from behind me.

"Two hours, fourteen minutes to go dreamer," informs the friendly voice.

"Done Terry?" I ask as I scan the insignificant skyline of the city.

"Done?" he responds. "I wish. Togo's tonight?"

I nod and he grins, then strolls back toward the other side of the building. I drop a fresh bag of gravel into the hopper, then lean against the hopper's tar-smudged handle. Other men share the warehouse roof, also waiting for the day to end.

"Ain't you go nothin' better t'do?" screams a crass voice.

"Does this face look like it cares?" I respond, well out of range from the foreman. The men step up their pace, moving around, some in circles, trying to look busy. I push the hopper across the roof a few times, also just going through the motions until he climbs back down the ladder. Immediately, some stop what they're doing and sit down on the freshly distributed gravel.

The sun inches back out from its hiding place as though trying to sneak from cloud to cloud without being detected. When the work day finally does end, it's down the ladder, into the car, on home, shower and onto Togo's.

I arrive before Terry at the small, unimpressive joint. The bartender serve me without exchanging a word, just as we've done countless times before. Yet, tonight I notice the pattern irritates me. Terry arrives eventually and accepts his beverage while I order a second with the easy sweep of a finger.

"Check that out," Terry motions with his head. Two young girls walk past, toward the jukebox. They look too young to be in here, moving freely in scant, loose-fitting outfits. Terry continues to study them, not silhouettes before the light of the jukebox.

We order another round. I sip the cool liquid in dismay, numbly watching the occasional activities surrounding me. Terry saying little, seems to be engrossed in his own small world. In his silence, glass in hand, leaning heavily against the bar, I detect a reflection of myself. The resemblance pulls me deeper into seclusion. How I used to look forward to these evenings, but now they blandly blur in with the rest of my obnoxious life, day upon day, year after pointless year. But then, it's always been that way with me.

I recall, even as a child, searching for a motive to ignite my life. Now I seldom looked if at all. The only things that progressed in my life were my age and my self-pity. In turn, I order another drink.

Melodies are cued from the jukebox. Girls flirt with hungry boys throughout the room. Just business as usual. Their occasional laughter imposes on my dark retreat. Terry starts complaining about the boss, or work, or his wife. His words bounce off my cloaked brain.

A tall, imposing man seats himself on the stool beside Terry. His voice is rough and rather deep. He orders a drink, then turns around and surveys the tavern, examining each individual closely. I glance his way as he accepts his drink then he turns towards Terry. He nods in greeting and smiles, displaying two rows of tarnished, discolored teeth. His thin, grey mustache curls with his smile and something in his stature reminds me of a swashbuckler I've seen on the late show.

Suddenly, my attention is diverted by the bartender, changing channels on the TV to a basketball game. Golden State at Cleveland. The Warriors are ahead, but I can't get interested. Something about the tall stranger gnaws at me. I've seen that ugly face before.

I look back. He's talking with Terry. I light a cigarette and listen in on their conversation. He shakes hands with Terry and writes down Terry's home number on a napkin.

Where have I seen that disgusting figure before? I lay my forehead on the wooden bar. The stranger finishes his drink and heads toward the door.

"Strange guy," Terry decides, turning back towards me.

"Catch his name?" I ask, setting upright.

"Yeah. It's – uh – uh, something strange. Begins with an A. Uh – uh..."

"Aquino?" I interrupt. My eyes are wide. My hands clutch the vinyl seat.

"Yeah," Terry responds, "Akeemo, or something like that. You know him?"

Terry's question barely grazes me as I race toward the door. Bolting into the dark streets, I am first greeted only by the cool, night air. Straining my eyes against the gloom, I sense panic, then see him, passing under a streetlight. I start to run.

"A-Q-U-I-N-O ! ! !"

The figure turns, still under the streetlight. As I approach, I see a hand, readied at his side and I stop running when I realize he's prepared to pull that huge knife his always carried.

"Aquino, it's me," I reassure. "Remember, ten-fifteen years ago? The boy you hired in Reno? We worked on your camper." I stop, still a few feet away, breathing heavily.

He studies me in the dim light, then his smile answers my inquiry. His hand drops from his knife and he steps toward me.

"How are you, boy?" he greets, grabbing both my shoulders with his strong hands.

"I'm fine. Getting along," I answer, excited and exuberant. We both pause, taking in the occasion. My mind recalls key moments from long ago.

I was eighteen then, traveling around the country by bus or thumb. Aquino and his family were living in camper. We met on a but to Reno where I agreed to work for him, repairing their truck. His wife, their teenage daughter Rachel and younger son Michal made up his caravan. The few, unusual days I spent with them climaxed when Rachel invited me to live with them as her husband the rest of my days.

"How have you been?" I request.

"Good, very good," Aquino announces, still smiling.

"How's Mrs. A?"

"Getting along," he admits.

"And Rachel . . . and Michal?" I hesitate.

"Everyone is fine, boy. Let me buy you a drink. Let us talk over those old times, then I must be home."

At first I accept, then "Wait! Could I possibly go back with you – for a bit? Just to say, 'hello' – to everybody - y'know? -- Do you think they'd remember me?"

"No," answers Aquino, solemnly. "Not while they sleep." He smiles again.

"Yeah, I guess it's sort of late. How about tomorrow . . . anytime?" I notice the urgency in my request.

"Tomorrow," he decides, "at that inn on the corner."

"Togo's? Great! What time?"

"You are working?" he asks.

"Uh-huh, and I get off at five, but I'll take off anytime if I have to."

"No, boy. You work. I will be there."

"Good," I approve. We face each other, not yet realizing this is the end of the reunion.

"It is good to see you again, boy," he adds, then turns to go.

"Can I give you a lift?" I offer. "My car's right over here." I point towards Togo's.

He shakes his head. "I will find my own way. Goodnight, boy." I remain under the street lamp, watching until he's out of sight.

The next day is obnoxiously long. Adrenalin skips through my veins bringing thousands of questions to mind. I feel like a child on Christmas eve who can't wait to discover the treasure under the tree.

When the painfully long shift finally does close, it's off the roof, home, showered and in Togo's by a quarter to six.

How the minutes tick by, transforming into hours, an eye constantly surveying the door. It isn't until closing time approaches that it occurs to me that I've been stood up. Aquino never intended to return.

"But, WHY?" I yell at the densely cool night air. Deserted avenues trail behind me as I walk from block to block, trying to console my frustrations. I wonder where they might be camped out, but Chico is a land of open pastures and farmlands. For all I know, Aquino could have packed up and moved on the minute he returned last night. He left me without even a hint toward their whereabouts nor any real details about them. I realized Rachel would surely be married by now and probably it'd be awkward meeting her husband. But, everything about that family was awkward. No doubt, Aquino chose to keep me away.

I find my car, start it up and watch hazy lights through the foggy windshield while the car warms up. The sound of the blower competes with the engine as I fearfully realize they've left me behind - again. The haze softens from the windows. I light up a smoke and head for the highway.

There's no tellin' which way they went," I remind myself, as the car enters the southbound thoroughfare. I study every vehicle within gloomy sight of the road. It isn't until the lights of Sacramento shine before me that I realize how far I've traveled. I pull off the road, opt not to spend the remainder of the night in a motel and drift back up to Chico.

The first wisps of light climb onto the horizon as I pull into a parking stall and head up the stairs to my apartment. Morosely, I enter my room, lay down on the couch and sadly fall asleep.

The cold, grey Saturday lumbers by. I lay around and watch TV, getting up only to change channels. I eat, but am not hungry. I want to escape this town, but there's nowhere to go. I want to weep while I try to convince myself its got to be better this way. Aquino and Rachel pass in and out of my thoughts until a knock at the door disturbs my vigil.

Expecting Terry, I cross the small room, open the door and almost drop when I see Aquino framed within the doorway.

"You were not hard to find, boy," Aquino explains from the passenger seat of my car. "I was needed at home last night and could not come. So, I phoned your friend and he led me to your doorstep."

"I'm glad you came," I admit.

"I know," he admits.

We enter and area of flat, open land, disturbed by intermittent trees and homes above the north side of town. A lone, old camper, parked next to a campfire, appears. Aquino directs me toward it and shortly we are alongside. Two large dogs immediately approach to investigate.

"Wait," Aquino directs and gets out to greet the animals.

I notice a surprising urge to leave, but grab hold of my fears and replace them with curiosity. I remind myself this isn't a homecoming and step into camp.

The dogs immediately approach, investigating by scent. One growls. Aquino calls them and they respond. A middle-aged man exits the camper.

"Aquino," he yells. "Where'd you go?" He's near my height, has darker hair and sunken eyes. He's dressed in blue jeans, flannel shirt and black boots. His beard is untrimmed and an obnoxious chain trails from a belt loop to his large leather wallet. He wears a knife similar to Aquino on his belt. He probably hasn't had a bath all week as his unkempt hair clings to his scalp.

"To town," Aquino answers, stirring the fire and placing another board on top.

"I toldja I needed help with the camper table this mornin'. Who's this?" he asks, warily.

"An old friend," Aquino explains. We worked together some years ago." Aquino studies the western horizon. I follow his gaze. The sun has just set. A wall of orange, red and violet trail behind, softly being absorbed into the land.

"Call Mama and Rachel," he turns towards Joe...

The man returns a defiant glance, then calls their names loudly.

"Do not yell like you call dogs," Aquino reprimands.

"I'm not your houseboy," the man confronts.

"So you say. So you say," Aquino calmly acknowledges.

The man walks to the door of the camper, opens squeaky hinges and climbs inside.

"Who's that?" I ask, wondering again if I should have come.

"Joe is his name. Rachel's husband. Calls himself a man." Aquino smiles and sets down on a box by the fire.

Then the camper door opens again. Two women, wrapped under shawls climb out; the first one very slowly. I immediately recognize Aquino's wife, though she is pale and has lost much weight. Grey streaks clash against her long, once jet black hair.

The second, younger woman helps her mother down. Clutching her shawl more tightly, she approaches. Her dark hair has grown considerably, but her face appears thin; perhaps haggard; perhaps sad. It was hard for me to believe this was the sensuous little angel, Rachel.

"Joe said you brought a friend," announces Aquino's wife. She looks at me briefly in the failing light, then sits on another box, next to Aquino. Rachel sits beside her mother and gazes at me across the campfire. Though I didn't expect it, I'd hoped for immediate recognition.

"This is the boy who worked for us many years back – in Reno," Aquino introduces.

Rachel looks at her father, then down at the blazing fire a moment, then suddenly she sits up and studies me more closely. It's hard to tell through the waving image what her reaction is, though she obviously remembers.

"Oh, yes," Mama exclaims and laughs, then a vaguely puzzled look enters her face. She turns to me.

"You are well?"

I nod and smile to conceal my insecurity. It's as thought I'm behind an imaginary partition looking in. The brief moment offers me a chance to collect my thoughts.

"I see you still cook over a campfire."

"Oh, yes," she repeats. "Truly, Rachel does most cooking. Especially now. The cold affects me so." She smiles lightly and scoots closer to the flames.

"Where do you go from here?" I ask.

"South," Aquino interjects, vaguely. "Winter can be too cold in our camper."

I recall nights past, by their campfire. Conversations had always been brief, though warm.

"Well, I must get back inside," declares Aquino's wife. "Papa, will you help me in?"

Aquino stands. His tall frame moves around her, placing a hand on my shoulder as he passes. He takes his wife in arm.

"You Mama looks like life's been rough on her," I sympathize.

"She's been very sick," Rachel confides. "I worry about her with the winter coming so quickly."

"How have you been?"

"Well," she says, abruptly, and gazes at the fire.

"I hope you don't mind my being here," I offer, being on my best behavior. "When I recognized your father in the bar, I wanted to see you and ----."

"Why did you come?" she interrupts.

I ponder the question carefully before answering.

"I'm not really sure," I decide. "I've thought about all of you often, especially you. Perhaps it was to find out some unanswered questions that bothered me all these years." A weak, reassuring smile comes to my face. Rachel nods, perhaps for me to go on.

"Like, I wondered, why did you all leave so suddenly?"

She appears disturbed that I would ask, but answers, "Because, - you – would not – have me. When you said 'no', there was no reason to stay. Papa wanted to find me a husband. Since you would not have me, we left to find somebody else."

"And that somebody else is Joe?" I ask, although the answer is self-evident.

She nods again, shortly, from behind the flames. "Perhaps we should not speak of the past," she confronts. Her stare is cold and unattractive.

I return the gaze, perhaps uneasily, then ask, "Can I ask you one more thing?"

Her expression remains a moment, then is disturbed by the sound of the camper door. Joe steps out and approaches.

I examine Rachel's reaction, difficult to perceive in the low light. Her lips tighten and she becomes anxious as he walks our way.

"There you are," Joe says and pulls up a box next to his wife. "It's getting' cold. Maybe u' better get inside."

She gathers her shawl tightly around her again, close up to her neck and stands to leave.

"Goodnight," we offer simultaneously. She responds with crunching footsteps upon the sand.

Then Joe turns to me. "She change much?"

I return a puzzled expression. "Yeah, I guess. Gotten older, like all of us."

Joe nods, kind of politely.

"Aquino's wife really looks different, though," I add.

"Yeah," he agrees. "She's not doin' too good." He stops and waits for me to add to the conversation.

"How long've you and Rachel been married?" I ask, as I realize I really don't care to talk with this weasel.

He stops, counts the years, then responds, "Oh, ten years, I guess. Can't never remember. Yeah. Rachel n' me've been together for a long time." He pulls his knife from its nest and begins to clean his fingernails. "Yeah, for a long time," he continues, "n' you get kinda close when y' been t'gether so long. We're easy with each other. Like t'keep it that way n' don't need no one messin' up our lives." He looks at my wavy figure through the heat. The shiny blade reflects the fire's glow.

A cold chill overtakes me and I fight to remain steady. I remind myself that I haven't done anything to threaten him. I only stopped by to make a social call. Maybe just to answer a few questions. Then, Rachel and Aquino could again become memories; history for my insignificant life.

Again the camper door opens. We both turn to see Aquino, raising up tall against the stars. The truck rises as he exits the steps. He moves around the far side of the vehicle, toward the trailer and reappears with a large case or something. Coming into the light, I see it's a sleeping bag.

"Care to spend the night, boy?" he addresses me.

I'm surprised by the offer but accept. There certainly is nothing at home to lure me, save perhaps my space heater. But then, that's all an open campfire is.

"It will be cold," he warns, "so keep the fire up." He drops the bag beside me. Joe scoffs and adds another board to the fire. Aquino, still standing, explores the beauty of the night sky. Most of the clouds have moved on. The rich darkness is packed with stars, glowing brightly through the clear atmosphere. Aquino is pleased by the fresh smell of the night. He reaches up and almost collects a handful of stars, then sits down as though leaving them for the rest of the world to enjoy.

I light a cigarette and flip the fresh ask into the fire. There's something reassuring about Aquino's presence which replaces Joe's precariousness.

We chat about the past years. I learn they've been all over the country, keeping mostly to the West Coast. Aquino's wife suffered a stroke two years earlier that almost stole her life. Michal, their son, was living in Sacramento. He also was married, had two children and laid concrete for a living. They visited him most often.

Halfway through the conversation, Joe unexpectedly rises and without a word heads on to bed. Aquino and I are left alone.

"Drink, boy?" he offers, pulling a pint of bourbon from his coat pocket. I accept. We both take a drink, then Aquino smiles. Even in the dim light, I notice those gross, discolored teeth, tarnished and old. We share another shot, then Aquino stands to leave.

"Do you need to return to town tomorrow?"

"No," I answer, then offer, "although if there's a problem with my being here...."

Aquino laughs quietly, though heartily. "You surprise me, boy. What problem could you bring that this tired life has not seen? The wind blows before all is still. Problems must come before there is rest." He pauses in the light of his poetry, then concludes, "I am not such a young man anymore. An extra hand would lighten my load. There is a shutter, broken, much like me, that is overdue repair. If you are able, tomorrow would be a good day to fix it." He winks and leaves the glowing warmth of the fire. A red bandana trails out from his rear pocket. Candlelight floods out of the camper as he opens the door. I can see his breath escape as he steps up into his home, so I throw another board on the fire, then lay out my sleeping bag.

The fire cracks and pops loudly. I lay entranced, watching it consume the wood. I feel the hard ground beneath me. I feel the cold, trying to claw its way into my sleeping bag. Moments later, my eyes close and with it, I sleep. I rest more deeply and more richly than I have in such a long time.

The following day passes much too quickly. Besides fixing the shutter, I repair a crack in the wooden roof of the camper and loosen a cab window that wouldn't roll down. I even silence the hinges of the camper door using oil off the dip stick of my car.

Rachel is a wonderful cook, much like her mother. The open fire is maintained throughout the day. Before I know it, the dinner is oven and everyone sits quietly around the fire, watching the active day steadily exit. Coats and long, wool shawls are retrieved. Aquino's wife is the first to escape the cool of the evening.

In the midst of fragmented conversation, I ask, "Aquino, why do you still live out of a camper?"

"What else would you have me, boy?" he replies.

"What I mean," I explain, "is it seems detrimental to your wife's health. I'd think she'd be better off more settled."

Aquino ponders an answer for some time, then says, "Perhaps I should agree with you, but this is where Mama wishes to be."

"Right after Mama's stroke," Rachel interjects, "we held a meeting. Michal was there. We talked it over with Mama and she decided this was where she would rather be." Rachel's manner is still cold and resentful, which was so much unlike her before.

Then, as though the final, exact moment had arrived, Aquino rises and heads for the camper. "Joe, I need your help," he requests.

Joe sits unmoved as we watch Aquino pace around to the far side of the van. Joe lazily stands, dusts himself off and follows.

"Perhaps I should go in, too," Rachel announces and begins to rise from her box.

"Rachel," I address, "please, could I talk to you a bit?"

"No," she decides. "There is nothing to say. If you have more questions, ask my father."

"What are you so afraid of?" I provoke.

She stares at me defiantly and proclaims, "I am not afraid of you."

"Then, why all the resentment?" I ask innocently, hoping to disarm her.

She sets back down, slowly, then demands, "Why did you come back here? Why do you stay so long?"

I briefly ponder a fair answer, and offer, "Can I tell you a small story?"

"If you like," she conducts.

I try to smile comfortably. "Once," I begin, "there was a lone man, walking along the beach. He saw a bottle washed up on the shore. He picked up the bottle, removed the old cork and suddenly a magnificent genie appeared before him.

'To him who has set me free, shall I grant him wishes three,' offered the genie, y'know. Well, the man thought for a moment then said, "Give me more money than I can possibly spend the rest of my life." And POOF!, suddenly money was pouring out of his pockets. The supply was unlimited.

Then the man said, 'Give me bigger, stronger muscles than any other man on Earth, and POOF!, he had this enormous physique. It ripped through the clothes he was wearing.

Then, the man, though pleased with his newly received fortune, began to fret, having only one wish left. So, he asked the magnificent genie, "May I wish for three more wishes?"

Well, the genie scolded him so severely for his greed that it upset the man who defended, "All I did was ask a question. I demand you take it all back," and with that, POOF!, the man was alone again, without money or muscles."

Rachel smiles slightly at the amusing outcome.

"At first," I add, "the man was shocked, y'know, as he realized what he'd said. He was struck with a great sense of loss that irked him the rest of his life."

Her smile fades.

"I felt like the man on the beach when you left. Now you and I both know I can never join your family. I had my chance and blew it, but I wanted you to know you all are like the treasure I came upon, then lost so abruptly. So, this short time with you has filled this hole that's haunted my life. You see what I mean?"

Rachel nods. A sad, apologetic smile sneaks onto her face, comforting those tight, anxious features.

"Remember the night you came to me?" I ask.

Immediately her manner stiffened.

"I promise you this is not bad," I reassure, but her expression remains.

"I tried to tell you last night. You're right, I did not say 'yes', to 'have you', but I never said, 'no,' either."

She appears puzzled and begins to protest.

"Now wait," I plea, "See, I wanted to talk to Aquino, to find out what I was enlisting into. That's all. But, I have to admit, I did a stupid job trying to tell you that. I'm sorry, because I'm sure I hurt you."

My apology surprises her and soon the golden fire glows in her moist eyes. I shift uncomfortably in my seat and notice a small tear trailing down her weathered cheek.

"I cannot believe this," she decides, her voice low and uneven. "The last time I cried over a man's words were in your tent." She speaks slowly and wipes the tear away. Immediately, another takes its place.

"Yesterday, I wasn't sure you'd remember me," I admit, and reflect that now she'll never forget me. "Have you ever relived that night and considered how it could've changed our lives?" My question would've been more out of place if I hadn't already dwelled on it so often.

She hesitates to answer, but responds, "Perhaps many times." She smiles sadly again, with much difficulty. "You were the only one who asked me of love. Perhaps I am funny, but that night, I was very much afraid of you, I think, because I was afraid of love. When I laid with you all night, I could not sleep...."

I scold myself for my selfish blindness, even if it is thirteen years past.

"I remember," reflects Rachel, "laying beside you with my hand on your chest, listening to your heartbeat. I hoped that you would awaken so we could talk perhaps more. But, I was afraid to disturb you. I know I cried much that night."

She picks up a board, stirs the receding fire, then drops the wood in its midst.

"My eyes were still red and ugly when I left you. I went to Papa and Mama and told them you said, 'No.' Papa asked me if we – if you – had me – made sex, like," she whispers, almost indistinguishable. "I had fear for your life. Perhaps I would have told him no, even if , , ," her voice breaks off.

Somehow I find myself thanking a God I never knew for helping me avoid what would've been my end. That lonely road on that cold morning suddenly sounded almost kind.

"Then?" I prompt.

She looks at me, rather embarrassed. "Then, we packed everything quietly. You did not move, even when we started the truck and I watched you out the back door until you were out of sight."

She looks down at her skirted lap and pulls her shawl securely around her shoulders. Both of us dwell silently in the moments that follow.

A chilly breeze passes over the rooftop, carrying dust and dirt. Occasionally, I glance over at the tear-off crew, unwind, prying large squares of old tar paper and rock from the warehouse roof. Loose gravel falls on the obsolete insulation, raising a cloud of dust which sails by us who recover the rooftop.

Terry and I help lay out large sheets of insulation on the swept, wooden surface. Others follow with tar paper, hot tar and gravel. Bit by bit, the long roof comes closer to being completed.

My mouth is dry from breathing dust. It agitates a chest cold which I've been trying to shake over the last couple weeks.

In the distance, I see an old camper heading south down the highway. Even from this distance, I can plainly see it's not Aquino and family. Reminiscing over them, I smile at the thought of Joe. How can I possibly remain angry with him for defending what was his?

Uncomfortable with leaving Rachel alone with me too long, he apparently sensed from the dark distance we were not simply chatting. I was not surprised to suddenly hear Joe and Aquino, still behind the camper, arguing, thought too far away to understand. Rachel tensed up, ready to help.

Then Joe approached, knife in hand. I grabbed an adequate board and stood behind the fire. Aquino also appeared, right behind him, also armed. He grabbed Joe's shoulder. Joe turned to break hold and swung at him with his unarmed hand. Aquino let go and backed just enough to allow Joes arm to fly by, then pushed him down to the ground.

While I stood there with my teeth in my mouth, Rachel ran, screaming, "STOP!" and stood between them. Joe jumped up and faced Aquino. His breathing was hard, probably from excitement.

"Stay out of my way, old man," he screamed, then addressed Rachel, "I ought to kill you too, slut."

Rachel extended an arm to touch his chest, but he batted it away. Yet, she persisted until he calmed down enough to accept her caresses. Again addressing Aquino, Joe declared, "I want him outa here tonight. Now! There nothin' else he needs 'n I'm not gonna watch him screw up my life."

Aquino nodded, approached me and suggested, "Boy, perhaps it is a good time to leave."

Still shaking and emotionally off-guard, my first thought was to try to patch-up differences with Joe. Then, the reality of his anger and my general sense of self-preservation took root and I dropped the board on the fire.

"I'm sorry," I responded to all three. Aquino escorted me to my car, knife still in hand.

"Thanks," I offered, closing the door, now safely within the metal chamber. "Thanks for having me – and saving my life. You can't imagine what it meant to me."

Aquino smiled at my nervous politeness. "Come when you can stay longer," he invited. My mind dissected his offer and I returned his smile.

"Say good-bye to Mrs. A," I requested. The engine was ordered into action and gears were engaged. I saw Rachel, holding Joe's head in her petite, calloused hands, perhaps scolding him, perhaps molding him.

That unreasonable sense of loss again haunted me as I left their humble camp. I lit a smoke and dwelled in the solitude of a lengthy drive.

The workday ends with obnoxious regularity. Driving home, I resist the temptation to drive by Aquino's camp; an itch which has recurred each evening, each morning, weekends, whenever. "Likely they're long gone," I reassure myself, but if not, I don't want to know. Such knowledge is better left untapped.

My car knows the way home. She beds down for the night and whispers, "Goodnight," through snaps and pops, as I walk up to my room. I drop off my tar-covered lunch box and head right for the shower, leaving a trail of filthy clothes behind me, alongside yesterday's trail. My occupation always requires a thorough scrubbing after each shift so Brer Rabbit won't mistake me for the Tar Baby.

[Shorter Ending]

I dry off, dress and find something for dinner. The TV is ignited and I settle down for the night.

Where I used to spend night after plastered night at somewhere like Togo's, clutching that glass like gold, that need seems to have left me. It still amazes me how much less stressful and less turbulent I am, but my world has become increasingly brighter. I even went to church. Imagine, me in a church. I don't know why I went, but I'm glad I did. My readjustments still require further growth, but I pursue it ambitiously.

Of course, I regularly reminisce over that family of nomads that brought me closer to myself. I miss them terribly at times, but realize my memories are not ones of loss, but rather, recollections of love. Occasionally, someone I meet reminds me of Joe, with his hot temper, weasel-like appearance and possessive fears. Perhaps I see Aquino, that ugly angel, always in control, turning the worst tragedy into triumph with calm self-assurance.

Most often, I see Rachel, gathering strength like driftwood on the beach with each trial set before her. Likewise, with each trial I encounter, I imagine becoming more and more like her.

An awful lot like her.

[Longer Ending]

After showering, I beeline to the kitchen, grab something for dinner and head to the living room. Suddenly, in astonishment, I come to a full stop. Rachel is there, curled up on my couch, beautiful as a portrait against the dingy interior of my living room.

Her smile greets my speechless bewilderment.

"I am sorry," she apologizes, still smiling. "you shower hid my knocking. Your door was unlocked, so I let myself in. Perhaps I did wrong?"

Finding my wits, I respond, "No, uh, that's fine. Where's everybody else?" I survey the rest of the small room.

"Papa and Mama shop for food before we begin our journey."

"Where are you off to, now?"

"South," she answers.

"Oh, well uh, can I get you something to drink?"

She smiles again, a mocking candor at my manners. "No, but that you. I did not come to drink."

"Why did you come?" I ask, seating myself in the lone chair across the small room from her.

"I might have come to say good-bye," she suggests. Then she sits up, stands, comes to kneel before me, takes my hands and adds, "but, that depends on you." She smiles again, though not so boldly.

"What depends on me?" I question, perhaps missing the obvious.

"I will try to explain," she begins. "Soon after you left, Joe went to town for two days. I think he went to find you; perhaps to hurt you; perhaps to kill you. I am not certain and Joe would not tell me.

"Still, as soon as Joe returned, we went to Michal's. Surely we needed to get away from you, but also, Michal could help. Joe always liked Michal. Even then, Joe still seemed angry and demanded to be left alone.

"So, last night, Papa, Mama and Michal and me had a talk. We see no other way than to have Joe leave."

"Why?" I ask. "Don't you think he'll get over it?"

"Perhaps," she admits, "but we see others like us who have tried. Their families were too often divided, or worse, someone was killed. We cannot wait to see. We will not let our family be broken."

"So, why are you telling me all this?" I re-ask, growing excited.

"Silly man," she chides. "We also decided to ask you to join our family." She stops, studying me for an answer.

I gaze into her soft, now anxious golden-brown eyes.

"Are you asking me to enlist into your family or be joined to you and with you, your family?" I interrogate, choosing my words carefully.

Rachel takes little time to respond. "I wish for you to be my husband, to live with me and take care of me, to shelter me and grow with me until one of us should die."

In the failing light of the evening, hands still clasped, Rachel kneeling submissively before me, I just about accept right there. I'd considered this moment countless times before and had accepted her each time. Even then, those were nothing more than cloudy fantasies. Here, reality was laid out before like a banquet table. I was anxious to dig in.

"But first, it's only right I should ask, "Is love included in the offer?"

She is openly delighted with my inquiry. "When you asked me of love years ago," she whispers, "I could not promise to love you. I was such a child," her grip on my hands tightens, "nor did I know how to love a man. I was angry when you came. It is easy to not love. But, I am not a child now. I have seen only a small part of you, but I know that I could love you."

As we cling together, simply enjoying each other, I am introduced to a sense of belonging and purpose, laced with love. She actually wants me, accepts me and cherishes me. But then as I hold this little angel close to me, I realize it's a lot like my feelings for her.

An awful lot like her.

An Awful Lot Like Us

13 Years Later

I've never understood change in a person's life. I mean real change; dynamic change; substantial change that goes beyond merely changing clean underwear. Perplexed, I wondered if some outside influence crashed through the mind, heart or soul to leave its destined mark or was the change always there, latently hibernating until some outside impression coaxed it out? I decided, if I found out, I'd have to let me know.

The times when I'd experienced change, I felt like dice exploring the crap table, never certain what numbers would appear while percentages promised I'd likely crap-out. Distrusting my selfish perceptions, my personal alterations never infiltrated the surface of my life any deeper than the ornate dots, carefully rationed throughout the red-blooded dice.

Occasionally, I yearned for that thaw which would warm and even ignite my spirit, but my heart always felt packed in permafrost, occasionally softening near the surface, but still soundly and securely frozen well within.

I've long believed every man possessed his own chill factor; those dispassionate barriers used to keep distance from others. In some, the chill factor was easy to spot, like when I'd visit those nice people at the light company or the IRS – especially when I was a month or so behind paying them. In others, the chill factor wasn't so easy to spot. I easily made a game of it, both as a sport and spectator, finding I could be as impervious as any bill collector. Yet, there struggled this languid voice inside me occasionally calling me to some accountability for my wallowing life. Always the hallowed against the hollowed.

I sipped temperate coffee, black and bitter. What had happened to me? I had been doing pretty well for a while – after they'd left. In fact, I'd been doing great. For the very first time I my life, I'd left the grave to walk the sunny surface, just like Jonah after the whale. I got out, met some people, tried to open up, rejoiced in some, got burned by others, almost married until she joined-up with the other torchbearers. Or maybe I carried my own destructive fire. It seems so stupid now. I found out how many of my friends were actually her friends. I also discovered how much I'd developed as I tried to retreat back into my waiting sepulcher, but wasn't the same man who'd emerged. Unexpectedly, it hurt to be parched and seared by life. Seeking conciliatory solitude, I found I'd lost that, too. Habitually, I lit a cigarette as coffee was reunited with my stained cup by a gorgeous waitress modeling a dumpy outfit.

"Where are they now?" I pondered aloud, smoke spattering each syllable. The waitress merely raised an eyebrow before hurrying away.

Strange. I hadn't thought much about Aquino or Rachel lately. They'd become less real over this last year, like characters in a story. Intimate, yet untouchable. I could retrieve the memories of our times together, but I couldn't deter or embalm their fading reality.

Consuming cigarette smoke, feeling it crash against my dead-end lungs, I watched bright-eyed automobiles amble by outside my window as I entertained the impossible quest to find them again. My caffeine enriched mind constructed my treasure hunt, trying to ignore the problem which threatened to deflate my bubbling enthusiasm, like someone across a crowded room I'd recognized, yet avoided, hoping they hadn't seen me. Yet, out of it came, how in the world was I going to find them?

Requesting my tab, I challenged myself to locate them. Racing down the road, I considered, evaluated and rejected most potential resources until the cloudy lights of Sacramento rose softly before me. Realizing how far I'd come, I stopped to turn back.

"But of course," I announced and dances with my left foot under the clutch. "Rachel's brother, Michal should have some idea where they're at. Maybe they're with him now."

Suddenly I realize I don't even know his last name. I did know he laid cement for a living in Sacramento, or had two years ago. It wasn't much, but it was a start. Beelining back to Chico, also realizing the late hour and that I had to work tomorrow, I wondered why I didn't think of him sooner. Finding his seemed remote, but improbability didn't disappoint me. Not yet! The following day, I called every cement layer in the phone book. "Michal" was pretty uncommon. I hoped someone would recognize the name without the last name, but I soon realized these suckers were as suspicious and tight-lipped as I'd be if they called me unexpectedly. I asked around my work to see if anyone knew any cement layers in Sac without headway. I called the union, but without a last name, nobody could help me. They graciously accepted my name and number.

I requested a week off work to roam Sacramento, big as it was. Even then, I accepted defeat as I gloomily realized it's been fifteen years since I'd seen him. I knew I'd have trouble recognizing him and resolved to find another channel to locate his family.

There was always this funny depression which enveloped me when I failed, yet I knew I had to continue to try. It was the same feeling I'd get when repairing my car, (poverty made me a shade-tree mechanic) and it wasn't going at all well, or I'd just spent hours fixing something which didn't really fix the problem, or right after I'd gotten it back together, I realized I'd left off some intricate part which required I dismantle it again. Someone'd told me, besides my frustration, I was experiencing self-pity. Fortunately, I'd never ventured to look within myself far enough to discover whether it was true or not. I wasn't interested in evaluating it, either.

I put-off my torturous search for a couple of days. The two short days soon passed a couple of weeks. I felt my sense of hope and preservation ebb away as I trudged through each day. The reasons for my search noticeably faded and blurred.

I called the union in Sacramento a couple more times without success. Without whispering the word suicide, its possibility crept up on me – or I crept up on it – or both crept together – or maybe I was the only creep. Terry, who hadn't called me in months, invited me to dinner.

"I don't know why you're so upset," he said, pouring a tall glass of wine. "They kicked you out last time. What're you gonna do this time? Just stroll into camp for a social call? Sounds like a death wish to me. What's-her-name's husband...."

"Joe."

"Yeah, Joe. I'll bet he'd love to see your old face again. How many times do you think he wished he'd at least knocked you around a bit? I'd bet anything he'd do it to you right next time."

"Easy to say, but not so easy to do," I defended, sort of poetically. "What's he gonna do? Walk up, stab me and I lay down and die? I don't think so."

"If he does, I wanna be there."

"Fiend."

"Friend."

Terry sat before me, with only the corner of his dining table between us, his near-empty glass protected with one hand, his fingers drumming the table with the other. The conversation lulled, its urgency softened by Tirolia. Terry refilled his glass. "I wish I could help you, man," he canted.

I nodded as he poured another tall glassful before me. Tangy and tart, the light fluid toured my palate searching for an escape, out and down, finding the gully of my stomach.

"You know, scrounge, if you dig a hole deep enough, everyone'll watch you jump in," I reminded myself, stewing as the wine and my denied self-pity ganged-up on me. Passively I studied the calm, pallid beverage.

"What's that?" Terry asked, tipping his ear.

"Nothing," I lied. "Sorry, but I've gotta go," I recomposed. I stood as I pushed the drink away. "There's got to be something I can do," I argued with both Terry and myself, "even if it takes a month , , , or another year. Then, after that I can talk myself into another year. But, I'm not going to find them sitting here."

"I still think you're making a big mistake, as one friend to another," plagiarized Terry, squeezing in between my thoughts. "And you'd be better off to just forget them."

I nodded, acknowledging a grinding justice behind his words, but expected there'd be time to forget them later. Then, unexpectedly, I saw Terry, like a malignancy or a cancer, trying to pull me back into my selfish mediocrity. He'd be my friend as long as I was depressed, broken and unstable. But, when I overlaid new wallpaper throughout the inner walls of my heart, Terry sought the company of those darker than I. I recalled hearing, a friend is one who stayed with you, not just when life was rosy, but when times were rough. That was the time to count your friends. If was a sweet thought – one I'd subscribed to, at least until now. Terry was the opposite; the photographer's negative; the inverse within my universe. The thought startled and repelled me.

I left Terry's, resolved to never return. I saw his at work, remained polite, avoided his ploys to get closer, never entertained animosity and persevered in my search. Weekly I called the cement-layer's union in Sacramento until they tired of me and as much as said so.

One weekend in mid-October, I drove up to Reno and found the campsite we'd first shared. As I yearned to come upon them, I set uninspired on the cold, hard dirt, barrenly empty, like my soul. Pitifully, I imagined pretty, young Rachel, helping her mama around the campfire or sensually removing a sliver from my finger. I recalled her delicate features in the candlelight of my tent and shuddered when I felt a small tear form in my own eyes, hosting a memorial.

A sharp, chilly wind stirred. Playing o favorites, it pushed through me; my bones still accustomed to the autumn of the lower valley. From my sandy seat, I sat gathering pebbles to play a quick game of "beans" with myself. As it happens, I lost the same game I won.

Whipping sand off my dirty clothing, I watched the dust drift down the road they took, leaving me alone and lost. It'd been too long. I'd taken too long to try to find them again.

I returned to Chico and stopped in Togo's for a beer, but it'd been so long. Nobody there I knew. Nobody there knew me. It was just as well. I'd only stopped by in case Aquino might've wandered in.

Then, from Chico, I went north. Not far. I found the second place we'd roosted. Unlike the Reno campsite, I'd been here numerous times, always driving by, but this time I stopped. The fire pit was still intact. Despite the lateness of the season, green spread out all around me like an ocean. It was beautiful and I'd completely missed it. The sun had set, so I gathered what wood was there and lit a small campfire. Shortly the stars joined me as I lit a smoke and watched the hungry flames.

Reflecting on friends, past and present, I felt Melancholy place one cold hand on my shoulder and Frustration take hod upon the other. I shook both of them off and tossed another stick into the blaze. Concentrating on the scalding warmth against my front and the scolding cold against my back, I scarcely noticed the headlights approaching. My heart leapt as the car stopped, ejecting one of the local cops. I stood to acknowledge him.

"Good evening," he greeted cautiously.

I nodded, wearing a tight smile.

"What brings you out here?" he quizzed.

"Memories," I admitted. There wasn't much rebellion stirring within me tonight. "A family I'd met camped out here a coupla years ago. I stayed with them, then. I'm just missing them now."

Usually abrupt with police, much like their abruptness with me, this tender, honest temperament fooled even me.

It apparently astonished him, too. "I'm sorry," he sympathized, then asked to see my drivers license. As he checked me out with the dispatcher, I resumed my vigil with my baby bonfire. It was getting late and I was getting tired. Tired of searching, mostly. Tired of disappointment. Tired of trying to remain optimistic, which I'd never excelled at before. I tossed my smoke into the red coals and watched it ignite the filter, first to flame, then to char.

The officer left me to my grieving peace. I'd had to many false alarms, I was becoming less tolerant. There were only so many disappointments I could put up with. I'd chased campfires all night or investigated campers for months now and couldn't help but feel discouraged. For the first time it seemed preferable to escape my insanity rather than continue the batter and search. In despair, I prayed. In prayer, I cried. My tears hopelessly tried to extinguish the fire. I dried my eyes, tossed sand on the embers and stirred them around. As I returned to my old apartment, I conceded to shelve my search, at least for a while.

After an insipid, uninspired week, I came to a full circle decision to give-up the search, hoping that someday I'd run into them again. A few days later, answering a knock at my door, I opened up to a uniformed cop. It took a long, laboring moment to recognize him as the same one who'd approached me by the campfire.

"Good news," he announced, entering my home. "I did some checking. We'd, of course, investigated some people in that vicinity a couple years ago. We received names, where I found them on disk. Computers are wonderful, aren't they?

"Anyway, I checked out other activity with these people and came up blank, except for one of their family; a man around your age who was arrested for drunken and disorderly. He jumped bail is still on warrant."

"Joe," I presumed.

"Joseph Briggs," he verified.

I'd never heard his last name. Then, I realized I'd better make sure we were discussing the same family.

"Can you name the rest of the party?"

He pulled a note pad from his coat pocket as he nodded. "Let's see. Aquino Rosen and his wife, Anna."

I'd also never heard his wife's name before.

"One grown daughter, Rachel Briggs."

"That's them," I assented, immediately getting excited. This was all going too slowly.

"Then I called Sacramento Metro on this Joseph Briggs. He'd been arrested a few ties for spouse abuse and assault. Sounds like quite the character."

I nodded. "So, have you caught him Do you know where they are? And, why're you doing this?"

He reviewed my small barrage of questions before answering.

"No, he's not currently in custody, as far as I know. Metro thinks they know where they are, although this man, Briggs, wasn't currently wanted in Sacramento County. And, I'm doing this because Jesus instructed me to."

The third answer pre-empted my evaluations of the first two. "Jesus, huh?" I challenged.

"I don't normally take the time to help people find friends. Families, yes. I could see you'd lost your family, even though you don't share the same surnames. So, during my off hours, I checked back, then sent out a general request. I got three responses. One from Sac Metro who'd thought they'd found them. Then, one from Susanville and one from Vacaville. If we get anything definitive, I'll let you know.

"As for me, I prayed about you after I'd left and Jesus seemed to tell me to follow-up with this one. I don't know why, but it doesn't matter why."

"I don't believe this. God never did anything for me," I challenged.

"Actually He did tons of things for you, but you apparently haven't noticed them. Besides things like life, intelligence, strength and health, He also sent me to you."

I looked at him, expecting the glazed stare of a lunatic. Instead, he spoke quietly, contemplatively and easily; his manner secure as a pickle in a jar.

"Yeah," he continued, "He sent me to you instead of someone like my sergeant. I've no doubt you two would've gotten along famously, but that's conjecture."

He offered directions to where they were last seen. The rest was up to me. He departed and I felt prismic gratitude mixed with selfish relief. It was bad enough knowing about God. I wasn't ready to get to know him, much less follow His ideals. I'd met too many self-appointed gods to be anxious to meld my life to any of them.

I shot off toward Sacramento, carefully following his directions. They were sweetly accurate and precise. My only mishap had been driving past the camp before I'd realized it was them. But, I'd been looking for an old, red camper, not a white Winnebago. This somehow didn't fit the box I'd always framed them within. Nonetheless, the drive-by provided an opportunity to evaluate them before approaching. The only reason I'd known them was when Joe walked out, glancing my way, but seeming fairly unconcerned, as far as I could tell. I kept on until I was out of sight. No hurry. I wouldn't lose them.

Soon the cool of the evening oozed in the open windows. I relaxed and took time to approach. I would've loved it if Joe hadn't been there as the reality of my adversary expanded. Strangely, I reconsidered the direct to approach them, feeling no hurry. There was no way I'd ever lose them. Not this time. Never again.

"I could call the cops," I listed, "or go fight him myself, or wait until he's gone or try to find

Aquino when he heads into town." I became less stressed at my list of relative options. I'd found them and, at least for right now, I had the ball. I fought off an unappreciated feeling of intrusion, like I was interfering with their lives, which suggested I leave them be. I lit a cigarette and watched the smoke drift up through my fingers, picking out swirling shapes before it escaped out the open window.

Waiting until nightfall, I left my car to creep in closer. I expected the dogs to be out so planned to not get too close. I watched the wind direction in true Tarzan form and approached accordingly. Exposed by starlight, I felt content to watch from any distance. Everything seemed too quiet or graciously domicile. Joe came out regularly, occupying the same seat by the fire as though it was his only friend. He cleaned muddy boots with his Bowie.

Then Aquino appeared, bold and confident, as I'd always seen him. His large silhouette first resembled pitch, backed by the candlelight. Yet, stepping from his home, the firelight reflected his dark eyes. He glanced at Joe, then took time to enjoy the night, overlooking the silent gloom around him. Looking up, he smiled at the ethereal pirouette of a billion stars above. I followed his sturdy gaze, his deep, piquant breath and his tethered, secured stature which covered that diamond-studded soul. Resenting Joe, still parked next to the campfire as he virtually ignored his father-in-law.

"How could he be so completely oblivious to the eminence of this man?" I wondered, suspecting Joe wouldn't give God the time of day.

Then, the motorhome door opened again. I prayed it was Rachel. God didn't disappoint me. She hadn't changed much since the last time I'd seen her. She still appeared church mouse thin. Her long, dark hair had grown. She donned her wool shawl and advanced to the campfire. Joe seemed to disregard her, too. I wanted to go over and punch him between the eyes; maybe straighten that pig nose of his. Aquino and Rachel conversed. Sadly, I was much too far to hear even an undistinguishable mumble. Then, I saw Joe's head go up. He spoke to Rachel, Aquino spoke to Joe, Joe rose, yelled, "Shut-up, old man," and stormed-off into the van, slamming the door behind him. It was nice to know things hadn't changed much in my absence.

Eventually, they all went in, lights inside when out and all became quiet. I waited alone another half hour, before creeping back to my car. Lighting my first cigarette in hours, I enjoyed the lulling freshness of the transparent night. Tossing the smoke, I laid back in my car to bed down for the remainder of the night.

"Thank You, God," I admitted. Setting up, I realized it was the first time I'd ever acknowledged personal assistance by any deity beyond myself. Oddly I detected a waned urgency to visit with them. It seemed more reasonable, as though merely seeing them was sufficient to again set me straight. It was incredulous life would be so simplistic; to take what life gave without disappointment, as though simplicity and life had anything in common. I settled into my warm front seat and, when I wasn't fighting the steering wheel, napped. Anxious for the morrow, I awoke often, wishing it were morning. At one point, impatient with the dragging darkness, feeling like a prisoner carrying out sentence within his dank cell, I set outside upon the hood of my car, counting stars while conducting the tenor hum of mosquitoes with the wave of my hand.

Watching the stars, I noticed a light rising beside an indifferent sky. Immediately, my adrenalin sparked. The long night was closing. I continued to welcome the light, delivered under personal invitation. Anxiously, I waited until the crescent moon peeked over the horizon. The nighttime was destined to continue, no matter how silly or anxious I felt. I childishly chided myself and crawled back in my car to sleep. Finally tired enough to relax, I found the timeless universe of sleep. I saw Aquino or Rachel, nonchalantly chatting with me as though I'd dropped in for coffee and biscuits with jam. I saw Joe, pounding at the door of their old camper, his muffled, distant threats demanding we let him in Aquino closed the shutters causing Joe's caustic image and voice to both dissipate. I immediately felt relief from tension I had not previously realized. I saw Michal, still twelve years old, yet sporting a black beard.

Then, they were gone. No, I was gone, out of the camper, in Terry's living room, telling him about my visit. He shook his head disapprovingly, then taunted, "You ran all over California looking for them and they were right here all along."

Quickly, I saw the entire family – no, there was only Rachel, sitting next to me on the floor, face to face, eye to eye, her dark hair knotted into a braid. Unhurried, she leaned toward me, as though to introduce a kiss. Carefully, I acknowledged the moment. I could feel her light breath sway my beard, about to touch when --- CRASH! Looking up from the ground, my legs still up on the car seat, my back smashed against the grassy ground, Aquino towered over me, his hand still on the door handle.

"Good morning, boy," he offered, enjoying my predicament. "You should have told us you coming. Come." He pulled me up with effortless control. Still heavy-headed with a sleepless hangover, I fought to come back to life. The fall hadn't helped.

"What're you doing here?" I croaked.

Aquino laughed, louder than I would've preferred. "Foolish boy," he toyed, "you steal my question. Come."

"Where?"

"Home," he permitted, leading the way.

I grabbed my cigarettes from the dash board and followed.

"Is it safe?" I asked and recalled that line from a not-too-old movie.

Aquino stopped to face me. "Does it matter?"

"I don't know," I admitted, as I felt my stinging senses trying to return. "You tell me. The last time I saw you, you'd just saved my life, or preserved it. As far as I know, the threat still exists and is ready to skin my hide anytime."

"I sent Joe into town. He never returns before evening, drunk or dead. He should not even notice you, or if he did, he could do nothing you could not stop. If we are lucky, he would be arrested again. Then, we could forget him for days, weeks or, if we are truly blest, months. He is a used tire, badly aligned, wearing out so young. He tires me. I am not so much a young man anymore. If he were gone, I would sleep better. Besides," he added, "you knew of danger before you came, yet here you stand, a boy. Perhaps a man."

"How'd you know it was me?"

"I knew you would come back. You surprise me taking so long."

"You're hard to find."

"And you are hard to miss."

"When did you know is was me?" I asked.

"I thought it was you when you drove by. I knew it before nightfall."

The morning was pleasantly cool, like it'd been picked fresh out of the garden. Aquino led, unhurriedly. We passed the knoll I'd held my sentry from last night. It looked smaller and less concealing under sunlight. The motorhome still seemed out of place. I'd expected Aquino would never give up his camper, yet if it was me, I realized this old motorhome would be my preference, too, even if it seemed out of character.

Then, the door opened. Rachel, thin and light, clung to the aluminum frame, watching me approach. Ready for any reception, my heart leapt when I saw her dance down the steps, prancing straight toward me, an embroidered smile dressing-up her face. Welcoming me with a hug, securely wrapped around my neck, I returned the unexpected embrace as a dream come true.

"Oh, I have missed you," she announced. "Where have you been? What took you so long?" Her arms remained tightly around me, wanted to never let go. "I always knew you would come back. You are staying, aren't you?"

Her mouth parked next to my ear, the invitation flew in as lightly as a cannonball.

"How can I, Mrs. Briggs?" I responded, biting my tongue, sadly crushing the moment.

She backed away – not too far and declared, "I do not care if I ever see that scab again." With viperous intention, she swore, "Everyday I hope he's dead. I would feed his bones to the dogs." She clung to my arm as she led the way to their home.

"Nice home," I applauded, winking at Aquino, climbing up the three aluminum steps. "Roomier than the last place. Must've cost you a bundle."

Aquino smiled behind that disgusting leer I always missed until I saw it again. "A gift from Michal," he boasted. "It is older and not so expensive. To us, it is a mansion on wheels. We now call it home."

"I expect you get social calls from Rockefellers and Kennedy's," I elaborated, borrowing an old tease.

"Speak what you will, boy. My papa would curse me for turning soft as he envied every inch of her. Come."

We set around a small table while Rachel served coffee; that bitter, black beverage which sweetened my every morning. Then, she sat down beside me, across from her father. I pulled out and lit a cigarette and allowed Rachel to lock onto my resting arm. My head cleared as I enjoyed my host and hostess.

Suddenly, a knot closed-in on my throat as I realized someone was missing. Where was Aquino's wife? I glanced around the room. Aquino detected my thoughts.

"She left us – last year. It was her time. She could wait no longer."

I closed my eyes in silent mourning for her, suspecting in some ways she'd been my favorite.

"I'm sorry," I pleaded.

Aquino nodded, ready to move onto any other subject. "Will you stay?" he asked, reminding me why I'd come.

"Get rid of Joe and I'll consider it." I answered, rhetorically.

"Is that not your job?" Aquino suggested.

Breathlessly I gazed at him, then out the window, overlooking the green and yellow grasslands. The sun insisted on rising, higher and higher, as though divinely inspired and unwilling to compromise those values. Its strength was motivating and I considered my probably options. I'd always hated fighting, especially if I was the one doing it.

"Well, let me make sure I understand you," I sidestepped. "I'd hate to make that same mistake again – asking for info and having it interpreted as a 'no'. Rachel set up, pouring part of her coffee in my lap and reset her mug. Facing Aquino, I ignored her abuse as the steaming liquid blanched my leg.

"Okay," I reviewed, "you're inviting me to live here with you?"

If you wish," Aquino acknowledged, going along.

"With you as my wife?" I asked, turning to Rachel.

"If you'll have me," she quipped.

"If I'll have you?" I repeated. "Silly woman. You have no idea how many times you've screwed-up my life. Every time I suspected I'd forgotten you and left you behind and finally said, 'Good-bye,' you'd surprise me, again breaking surface. My poor heart never could completely let you go, mostly because it never really wanted to. Of course I'll have you. I don't know how to love anyone else."

Like an iced tea glass on a hot day, her tears seeped, soaking her softened eyes, reflecting the sunlight through the windows.

The sun drifted overhead, scattered countless photons as we spent a quiet, pleasant day, chatting, playing and working, ever watching the road for Joe's return. Expecting to tangle with that problem when it arrived, I decided spontaneity had its preferred facets.

We dined around the campfire as the evening rested against our scorched, thirsty nerves.

"Any idea where he is?" I asked Aquino after Rachel had gone inside.

A vinegary smile seeped up the side of his tight, tanned cheek as yellow flashes rebounded off his face beside the flapping wings of the campfire. With that voice like soot, he croaked, "Drunk – again, or arrested – again – or both. He is a housefly – aimlessly flying, changing direction without plan. Unable to see behind him. He his gravel under angry tires. He shall never return or he is here now, watching. We cannot tell and we cannot see him coming." Aquino stood, firmly pressing down the ground as he left me wondering.

As he stroke to his mobile cabin, I hastily strolled around to the back of the van, out of the campfire's light. Rachel must've heard me for she came out with a warm, wool shawl wrapped around her shoulders, trekking directly to me. We sat on the wide, seatlike bumper as she took hold of my hand.

"How did you and Joe meet?" I questioned.

"Why do you ask such things?" she scolded, her eyes cutting through the darkness.

71

"Just curious. No, it's more than that. Maybe I see myself in Joe's place. If I was losing my wife, my home and my livelihood, all at once, I'd be pretty upset. But, if you don't want to tell me, that's okay, too."

She shifted uneasily beside me. I squeezed her hand to comfort her.

"After we had left you, I was afraid," she recalled. "Angry and afraid. Sometimes I think I picked the angriest man I found. Papa let me go to the coffee shop in the bus station in Reno. Joe took a table by me. I did not like him, but I made a smile. He started talking to me. You remember how shy I was. I did not dare interrupt him and he kept talking. Now he never talks at all." She gazed at the dark, shaded footprints molding the Earth around them.

"When he stopped drinking coffee," she murmured, "I asked him where he was going and he said Vacaville, so I offered him a ride. He rode with us and Papa got to talk to him. I know Papa did not like him at all. Now I know why. From there, it was a lot like you. He camped out with us and never left. After a few nights, I went to his tent. The next night, he moved in the camper." She kicked a rock out onto the dirt road. Following the mild squeak of door hinges, Aquino dropped down from the truck. The bumper raised slightly.

"Do you still love him?" I quizzed.

She glared at me. "I never did love him. Until you came last time, I did not know I was able

72

to love. For me, love was barren, like my womb. Without you, I would never learn..."

Her eyes closed to mourn. Her features softened, disguised behind blank, mindless shadows, cradled in sadness.

"Wait!" I interrupted, setting up. "You say Joe just moved in?"

She nodded. I jumped up, excited.

"So, you never got married, you know – through a preacher or a justice-of-the-peace or something?"

Her eyes grew and a small smile appeared. "Why?" she asked.

I jumped up and danced around the grounds a few times, excited for the first time in my life. I grabbed Rachel's hands and pulled her up, swinging her around a few times. She resisted, unaccustomed to being played with and pulled away until I picked her up and swung her around an unaccounted number of times, still elated. Her long dress flapped in the breeze like a flag. Then, setting her down, I gasped to regain my breath. Taking her hand, I classically knelt and requested, "Rachel, will you marry me?"

Rachel only stared at this madman, so I explained, "There's no common law marriage in California – or Nevada. That's why there's all those palimony suits in this state. But for us, there's no real estate or children to muck things up. You're free. Joe has no legal rights to you. So, before he does come, I want you. I want you forever. I wish I'd thought of this earlier today. We could've gone into town and got married this afternoon; this morning. We could've invited Joe. What do you say?"

Shivering with an unacquainted wave of emotion and excitement, she pressed her hands against mine and responded, "Yes, of course I'll marry you. Will you marry me?"

"The sooner, the better."

Then, that laugh, like rocks falling, led the way as Aquino appeared. "Well done, boy. If you ever leave us again, I'll probably kill you." It was an odd way of welcoming me into his home, but I took no offense.

"The only reason I'd leave is because you two were dead," I committed.

"Good," he applauded and pointed, "and now you'll have a chance to tell Joe for he comes."

I turned toward the dark road and released my hold on Rachel. She took position behind me. I had no weapon, no plan, no nature to fight, nor could I see him. However unready to face my adversary, I prepared, until I heard Aquino laughing heartily behind me.

"Now I know how fast you can jump," he guffawed.

"Very funny," I scolded, just realizing the joke.

"Oh, Papa," Rachel joined, certain she should have known better.

"Forgive me, boy," he requested, rubbing his left eye. "I promise I will not be Peter again. Now I know you would stay to fight."

Suddenly, I wanted to stomp him. I was readied for a fight anyway. Maybe I'd divert my revived adrenalin on Aquino. It'd serve him right and give me something to do with all this invested excess energy. Rapidly pacing around the grounds until I simmered down, we reluctantly returned to the obnoxious watch and wait.

Kissing my wife-to-be goodnight, I set down near Aquino by the campfire.

"What do you think?" I asked Aquino, smoldering with anticipation.

"Joe has been gone all night before," he responded. "Like a tomcat, he will carouse. I pray for the whores he finds, that they will not bear his sons. Go in to bed, boy? Rachel will surely awaken for you."

"Maybe I'll go in to say goodnight," I preferred. I departed the incredible peace and beauty of the full sky of stars spread all the way down to the fresh, rippled horizon. Each creak grit my teeth as I crept near Rachel, content to review the day in the peace of the night. Like a pinch, I knew I wasn't dreaming. Yet, a strange sadness toured through me as I watched my slumbering angel. Like a grudge, I hated the time lost.

"Who's there?" Rachel hissed.

"Just me," I comforted. "Are you okay?" It wasn't until she moved that I could see her.

"Fine," she smiled, yawning lazily. "I guess Joe is not back?"

"No," I nodded, "and I wish he'd get here. I was anxious before. Now I'm ready to be done with it." I rose.

"Where do you go?"

"Just back to my car for more cigarettes. You go back to sleep. I leaned to kiss her forehead. Passively accepting my peck, she unexpectedly grabbed hold of me and pulled me on top of her. We spent the next few moments kissing and touching. In an expression as old as mankind, but freshly kindled within us, she soon began undressing me and herself, until I stopped her.

"What?" she asked, responding defensively.

Nothing, my love," I wooed awkwardly, "but let's way until after we're married."

"Why?"

"Lots of reasons. Legality. I'd rather be actually married first."

"And I could not care however. I do not need some piece of paper to hold me to the one I love."

"But, it's not just paper. It's a testimony to a covenant, between you and me. A partnership until death does us part sort of thing. It'd be like baptism to a Christian; like initiation in high school or the dorms in college. You don't have to do it, but it makes it real. You've decided today where you will start and you've decided where you're going."

"I still think you foolish," she pronounced, licking her wounds.

"Okay, consider this," I continued, "Relationships are built like a building. The couple together lays foundation, then constructs the building from there. You built on a flimsy

76

foundation with Joe and look what happened. I was vacant. It was hollow. The foundation crumbled and the structure fell with it. You two are going through the motions but you're living in the ruins. You can reconstruct, but so far it seems you haven't done much."

"What makes you think you know what Joe and I started?"

"Didn't you tell me you were angry; that you felt rejected?"

She bowed her head toward the bedcovers and whispered, "Yes."

"Then, you built your relationship out of fear. Fear of rejection. It didn't matter whether you liked him or not. It didn't matter if he liked you or . . ."

"STOP!"

"I'm sorry," I apologized while nearby crickets serenaded for a mate and cicadas whistled a happy tune. "Really," I insisted. "Sometimes I get carried away. I took a couple courses at U. C. Chico, so I'm just parroting what my instructor taught. Uh remember that night when you came to my tent – the first time when we were just kids?"

Rachel's defenses softened as she turned to me.

I continued, "I've relived that night at least a thousand times, I'll bet, y'know. One of the things I remembered thinking while you were sitting there making my whole stupid world sound rosy was that you offered to consummate the relationship before it happened."

"What is consum-mate?" she asked, awkwardly.

"Uh, I've always heard it as having sex after your get married. Like you're not actually married until you've made it, y'know." I smiled sheepishly, wondering why, no matter how easy it would've been to consummate here and now, it was still commonly embarrassing to talk about it.

The squeaky door announced Aquino's entrance.

"Talk, talk, talk. I need to sleep." He set down to pull his boots off.

Kissing Rachel, I reported, "Let me run back to my car. I be back in a few minutes."

"Promises. What good are the promises of a tease?" she teased.

Smiling, yet incredulous at my own scruples, I stepped down into the brisk, late night, early morning. Every star turned to look at me, brightly curious. I buttoned up my old chambray shirt as I strolled down the dirt road towards my car. A crooked crescent moon sadly rose, yellow and dreamy. It added enough light to my trail to keep me from stumbling.

Rounding the worn down knoll where I'd spent much of last night, I detected something – a dark figure running at me, here, upon me, boom, he collided with me, trying to be a freight train on the flat face of a semi bound to smash me down.

I caught the metallic reflection of moonlight flash across a knife blade. It nothing else, I'd stop that blade from at least one advance.

Years of pushing tar and gravel on rooftops produced some great muscle tone. Joe rammed into me, but I didn't move very far. Stumbling, I kept my feet. He swung his knife a couple of times, well out of reach, then lurched mid-chest. I jumped aside, grabbing his arm instinctively and began swinging him around like a spider on a web. Conveniently avoiding the blade, still tightly within his grip, I swung him around me at least a couple full revolutions, picking up speed and momentum. To stop, he fell to his knees, skidding against the ball bearing gravel and dirt, and I was on him. Keeping hold of the arm, I used it to tip him off balance, then planted myself on top of his chest, my shins pinning down his shoulders in a hold I'd used dozens of times to torment my younger brother before feeding him his old, dirty socks while he yelled for mom. This opponent had been no more of a match than my wimp brother.

"Get off of me," he yelled, struggling hopelessly.

"Let go of the knife," I commanded.

"Get off of me," he repeated, insanely furious; snared and helpless; too stupid to realize his predicament.

"you drop that knife, or I'll beat you within an inch of your life," I bluffed, "and once I get started, I never know if I can stop."

"I'll kill you, sucker," he screamed. The hot aroma of beer pounded against my face.

"Not without my permission," I taunted. "Now drop the knife. NOW!"

"I'll kill you," he squawked again, his voice cold and hoarse.

Rachel and Aquino approached, running. Identifying who was on top of whom, Aquino, his knife dangling from his hand, took time to enjoy a good laugh.

"Boy, half my kingdom is yours," he croaked. "Would you like some help?"

"Yeah. Get the knife out of his right hand."

Writhing for freedom, Joe yelled, "Touch me and I'll kill you, Aquino."

Still chortling, Aquino came around placing the heel of his boot firmly against Joe's wrist and palm. Crushed into the rough ground, Joe's hand squirmed, releasing its hold. Joe weaponless, I asked, "What do we do with him now?"

We could execute him – with his own knife," Aquino suggested, holding it up, ready to sharpen it off the rough edge of the moon.

I wouldn't be an execution if it's self-defense," I remarked. "He's history whether he departs in one piece or many.

Joe struggled to turn over again but remained helpless against greater weight and strength.

"We could have him arrested to serve time on his warrants. I'm sure the police would love to consummate this case." I looked up at Rachel and smiled. There was that word again.

"Get off me," he demanded. "I can't breathe."

"Shut-up," I ordered, my mouth barely inches from his ear.

"You go to Hell."

"No, you listen. It comes down to this." I found myself yelling; my hot breath condensed against his sizzling face. "Your life here's through. Even if I leave, (and you can be sure I'm not), you're no longer welcome."

Joe, trying to avoid my glare, caught sight of Rachel.

"Slut," he clamored.

Suddenly, fearfully enraged, I smashed my fist against his defenseless jaw. "Shut-up," I screamed. His hand free, he immediately calmed down, finally feeling the weight of his predicament.

"You can pack-up and move on or I'll turn you in right now. I'll hog tie you and toss you in my trunk and drive you right down to the station. I'm not messing with you anymore. Tonight's little attack could be construed as an attempted murder. Now what's it going to be?"

"Get off me and I'll tell you."

"Tell me now or I'll take you in, Joe Briggs."

He scowled and repeated, "Get off me and I'll tell you."

"Aquino, do we have any rope?"

"Of course."

"Okay. Okay," resigned Joe. "I'll leave. Just get off me and I'll leave."

"Peaeably?"

"I'll leave peaceably."

"Never to come back?"

"Yeah, whatever. Just get off me."

I rose carefully when stood back as Joe pulled himself up. He brushed off his clothes as he headed toward the motorhome.

"Keys," Aquino announced. Joe pulled out his key chain, removed two keys and tossed them into the night.

"Find them yourself, sucker," he challenged.

Aquino glanced at me, coolly in charge. "No, thank you," he politely responded, turning toward the van, slightly motioning for us to follow.

"Where do you think you are going?" demanded Joe, disrupting the songs of the night.

"Where do you think you are going?" retorted Aquino.

"I need to get my stuff," Joe snapped. "Is that alright if I get my stuff?"

"If he tries to take even one step inside that van, I'll be right back on top of him," I assured Aquino.

"Wow! Big man. I'm really scared," taunted Joe, holding down the ground behind us.

"You're also really stupid," I stabbed, turning back towards Joe.

"Oh, and why and I stupid?" he spit.

"Because you're free," I explained; a barebones silence pausing between my words. "Here's a chance to restart your life. You've never been happy here. Get out. Why prolong it? You've known it's been trashed for a long time. You only stayed 'cause it was convenient and you were too lazy." Joe scoffed, kicking gravel as he followed.

"Take what you want," Aquino planned out loud. "We will take the rest of Michal's. You can pick it up from him."

Joe selected a few items and a pack. "Can I have my knife back? I'll probably need that more than anything else here."

Still fingering the large blade, Aquino whittled the air briefly before flinging the impressive knife, straighter than a football, into high grass and trees. "Find it yourself, sucker," he duplicated, a hard, intense smile against his hard, strong face.

Grumbling, Joe placed his pack on his back, shifting the weight until it was comfortable. Walking by me, he snarled, "How does it feel to get a used woman?"

"Once you get past the used part, pretty good," I countered, eye for an eye.

Shaking with rage, ready to erupt, he somehow maintained, his teeth clamped tightly as he walked into the night. All watched him disappear, uneasily certain all was not settled. He'd surely turn up again.

"It is time to go," dictated Aquino, kicking dirt on the simmering fire.

"We are always ready to flee," Aquino explained as we drove out to pick-up my car, bobbing between the pitch and the sway of this large box upon an unpaved road. As the headlights found my car, I examined it for tampering and was pleased to find none. It started right up and (relatively speaking,) drove perfectly.

"Where to?" I called to Aquino, hanging half out the open door.

"Chico. Your place," he yelled. Wait." Turning to Rachel, he offered, "Do you want to ride with him?"

Rachel gazed out the wide screen windshield, shocked the idea hadn't occurred to her first. Crossing the brief distance to her Papa, she hugged him, affectionately bit his ear and grabbed her shawl as she hopped down, pranced across the beams of headlight and waved before ducking into the car.

Setting like a king in his high-backed captain's chair, habitually swiveling back and forth, his weathered arms resting on the steering wheel, Aquino watched his baby angel dance away from him. Shuddering down to the toes of his soul, he hosted a deep, endemic affection towards his sweet daughter. Delightfully, he watched as he tried to recall the last time he'd seen her this happy. But, his joy was twisted by an anxious fear of loneliness. Like Michal, Rachel may prefer to settle down with this boy, leaving Aquino alone to roam. His face a tail-light red, he angled the rear-view mirror to look at himself.

Though intact, a cracked and crooked trail crossed the glass he now used to reflect upon his life, past and present.

"There's no fool like an old fool," smiled Aquino, feeling sophic, leering at his crimson reflection. The large van pitched sharply tossing Aquino like flotsam aboard the stormy waves. Supporting himself with the steering wheel, he eventually piloted onto gravel and pavement, still keeping pace with the car. Rolling onto the highway, he picked up speed as it sportingly occurred to him the hadn't seen Joe along the long dirt road.

As quickly as they'd packed up, Joe couldn't have come this far. "Like a snake, he probably hid in the grass," Aquino guessed. "And, like a coward, he rides with us now." He looked back through both mirrors quietly calculating an opportunity to check with minimum risk. Aquino laughed to himself through sleepy eyes. Let him hold on for awhile if he wants to ride along. He will find it's harder work and not much fun.

Meanwhile, Rachel and I enjoyed the tie getting to know each other. The crescent moon hung above us like a dentist's smile. Jupiter had appeared to the east, celebrating our homecoming by outshining the accompanying stars. Rachel peered out, overlooking the nocturnal landscape. Looking over at her, I saw her face reflected in the window, illuminated by the instrument panel. She caught me monitoring her, indicated by her mirrored smile, and we were both reminded how incredible this all was.

"Tired?" I asked, seeing her yawn. It'd been a long, intense day. The late hour was wearing on both of us. I fought the same yawn which had jumped from her over to me. She cuddled next to me and nodded.

"Having any second thoughts?"

"About what?" she responded, setting upright.

"About us," I offered, almost casually, not really worried.

"Are you?" she blistered.

Initially bewildered, I soon discovered how I'd become accustomed to dealing with indecisive, bartersome creatures versus this woman who'd probably never second-guessed a decision her entire adult life.

"Of course not, silly woman," I chided promptly, "but what if you'd said 'take a hike, jerk. We ain't going through this again.'? What could I've done, then? The last time I came, you were pretty icy the first couple of days. What if things had gotten better between you and Joe?"

"But, they did not..." she announced, sharply revoking the latest question.

"Can I ask you something?" I plotted. Not awaiting her answer, I pursued, "What Joe - uh - abusive?" Still setting upright, she remained silent. Initially guessing the worst, I reconsidered that she probably didn't understand the question.

"I know you had arguments," I restarted. "Did he ever hit you?"

Quiet and still, the clinging caress she'd maintained and nurtured on my arm throughout the journey conspicuously halted. Immediately aware I was treading through dangerous territory, I spoke carefully, yet deliberately. With the mindfulness of an explorer, I attempted to explain, "I want you to understand something.

I'm not Joe. I'm here cause I want to be - mostly out of love for you. Today all my dreams came true. I can't wait to see where they'll take us." I brushed my fingers through her long, sable hair, trying to reassure her; fearful she'd perceive my affectionate approach as a trap.

"So," I gambled, "my guess is that you fought - a lot, and that when you weren't fighting, there wasn't a lot of loving. I also suspect he hit you. No, now that I really think about it, he must've beat you, more than once, and that you'd probably be dead today if your father hadn't been there to save you."

I detected a bare nod from the peripheral corner of my eye.

"He almost killed me," she choked, "many times."

Covered with goose bumps, I turned up the heater, privately wondering what I'd do if I have him pinned to the ground again. Softly covering Rachel's far cheek and ear, I leaned toward her to kiss the side of her head as she sobbed, deeply and piteously.

Passively, I lit a cigarette as we approached Marysville. As the old highway metamorphosed to interstate, Aquino accelerated, passing us. Then, when safely out front, floated over in front of us. Instantly, Rachel and I saw the freeloader clinging to the back of the caravan.

I flashed my headlights off and on, hoping Aquino would understand. Aquino flashed his amber lights in response. Joe looked back and around, as though there might be somewhere to escape to. At sixty plus miles per hour, his options were limited.

Racing to come alongside with Aquino, Rachel rolled down her window.

"What now?" I yelled, my words filling the chasm inside my car, but falling far short of Aquino's ears. Rachel repeated the question.

"Chico," he yelled, pointing directly in front of him. "Does he have his pack?" Aquino researched.

Rachel affirmed as she yelled, her words barely able to cross the raging river of wind flowing between the two vehicles. Aquino appeared to have heard, smiled and nodded, motioned forward with his hands like a novice guiding a jumbo airliner to its gate. Laughing inaudibly, he eased up, allowing us to retake the lead and settled back for the rest of the late night ride.

Realizing the night wasn't over yet, my mind went on ahead of our caravan to scout the first stop off the highway, while offering Rachel, tearful and angry, my assurances.

Even then, I knew that all my considerations and plans would be hopelessly inadequate against the uncertainty of Joe's intentions. Even Rachel admitted she feared the worst, then added that Joe had great night vision. Perhaps he'd found his knife in the tall grass while they were retrieving the car.

The road immediately becomes long and foreboding; the time a shivery pain as the pleasant, sleepy intimacy they shared was dumped out onto the cold, flowing pavement below.

Surprisingly, right on schedule, the exit arrived; a curly ribbon road with merged with another highway into town. Looking around, I decided this would be the best place to conduct the showdown. I signaled to pull over. Aquino signaled behind me. We both grabbed the shoulder together.

After two seated hours and the intense, long day, I stiffly jumped out of my car and attempted to run back.

Aquino dropped down as well, knife in hand and yelled, "Around the other side, boy."

Immediately I diverted, between the vehicles. Rachel. He'd come up the passenger side to attack Rachel. She was just climbing from the car as I "cautiously" jumped out from the front of the van.

I tried to come up with a word to describe the blended feelings of relief and disappointment when I didn't see Joe. Unsuccessful, I sprinted back to where the first armed figure I saw was Aquino, surveying the area. It was obvious Joe hadn't yet come up either side. The surrounding weeks and growth were thick enough to conceal a man. Rachel caught up, taking position between us.

Another car exited, exposing Joe, crouched down, fifty yards behind the motor home. He still wore his pack and made no effort to rise.

Aquino and I walked aggressively toward him, still ready for a fight. My anger and tolerance were at opposite ends, stretched tight, wound-up, ready to spring. Aquino and I maintained a strategic distance, ready to cover either flank. We approached with the caution hunters use to approach wounded animals in the wilds.

Another car exited and I saw Aquino stop and fold his arms, conveniently concealing his knife. The car flew past. He continued. I continued.

Joe seemed oblivious as we stalked. Closer, I saw he was sitting on the sand and gravel; not crouching. He was cursing under his breath, but it sounded more like despair than anger. He also emitted sounds which resembled sobs. Aquino dropped his arm. His knife dwelt quietly as his side. Joe continued to weep, his tears reflecting the red taillights. Many minutes passed before he tried to stand, but his legs were wobbly, probably from the long, demanding ride on the tailgate. He writhed, driving muscle pains from his back. He was scraped up and covered with dirt and rock. It appeared that he'd jumped as soon as Aquino began to move off the asphalt but found his legs unable to compete with the speed of travel and over he went. I noticed a wide scrape across his right arm, smeared with blood coated under black dust. Rising, he used his backpack as a cane to steady himself. Brushing off the dirt and drying his eyes, he finally acknowledged us.

"I don' know why I did it," he confessed, looking at Rachel. "I don' know if it was to kill you or ask your forgiveness. I coulda done both. Now I can't do neither. I just – I just – I jus' don't know. I was walking. I saw you coming, so I laid in the grass. I though you'd saw me, but I hopped on anyway. I thought maybe . . ." Tears returned to his eyes. His voice choked as he continued, "What'm I gonna do? I don' know where to go. I ain't been home in years. My wi- ... I don' know where to go now. I feel like some total jerk. I jus' wanted to . . . Rachel?"

Rachel took a small step forward.

"Rachel, baby. Don' leave me, honey. I ain't perfect, but I ain't all bad neither. You know I can't be alone." He gulped, "Don' make me hate you. I know you better'n anyone else. I'll die without you, baby. I've changed. I'll change. I promise I'll be a better man." He shuddered with pain. "Oh, God! Why do I feel this way? Oh, God! Kill me now. Please just trash my life."

Rachel stepped forward to put a hand against his cheek. Joe's dark, greasy hair flopped over his face, which he pushed back; the gravel plastered to his bloody hand.

"Why'd you leave me? Was I really that bad? If it was so bad, why'd you stay with me so long?"

I stood pitifully afraid I'd lose her again. Wanting to yank her away, back to me, I planted myself. It had to be her choice – forgiveness or good-bye. I bit my lip anxiously. Looking over at Aquino, I bit down ever harder – puzzled briefly before I realized he held stance, ready to strike, understanding the danger of this vulnerable position.

Joe accepted her caress as he dried his tears. Pushing his hair back again, he looked at her through drained, hollow eyes, sadly begging forgiveness. As Rachel offered consolation, he reached to take her hand.

Meeting his gaze, she retreated, pulling away, simultaneously taking a step back.

"Baby," he whispered, reminding her again of an old pet name they once shared.

"No, Joe," she nodded, taking another step back.

Joe straightened up, responding to her answer. Sadly, he nodded as he mounted the pack he'd used for support. As the subtle light of dawn moseyed over the flat, low horizon, he met my eyes and spent a long moment examining them. I expected hostility, or at least resentment. Instead, I faced peacefulness – a quiet acceptance; one I didn't understand. Guessing I simply didn't know him well enough, I turned toward Rachel who looked equally puzzled. Somehow she'd never seen this side of his, either.

"Take good care of her," he ordered as he took a step backwards to begin his trek to the highway.

Alone, I suddenly felt very tired and yearned for a bed; any bed. Aquino rubbed the sleep from his eyes behind me as he turned toward his home.

"Let's go, boy. Lead the way or we sleep here."

Rachel accepted my tug, watching Joe one last time. We beelined to my pad. We flew to our beds. We hurried to sleep.

Come mid-afternoon, I awoke to the sound of someone in the kitchen. Not accustomed to sounds in my apartment, I arose, stumbling out to find Rachel, pouring coffee and shaking her head with disgust at the junk I called food lining my cupboards.

If this is what you eat, I do not know if I want you," she scolded.

I smiled and took my favorite seat as she served a most welcome cup of coffee. I gazed out my window toward the motorhome. Everything was still. I expected Aquino was still asleep.

"Papa went into town for supplies," interrupted Rachel.

"Oh, then I'm the last one up?" I said as I realized it was unpardonably still to presume otherwise. Rachel only smiled – an easy curl nudging up one cheek.

Soon Aquino returned, jovial and brash. "You have much fine stuff," he announced. "All of it is yours?"

Looking briefly around the house, both with my mind and my eyes, I nodded.

"Good," applauded Aquino. "Then we have much to sell."

"But most of it is just junk," I rated.

"You bought it, did you not?" Aquino bantered. "You have been to the flea markets; the yard sale; the swap meet? Though there are many things I do, many trades I perform, I am a sad man when I cannot sell. Or buy. Joe could repair anything, but he never learned to barter. I hope I can teach you."

I felt oddly threated, and tried to smile, forcing a standard of relative trust. I disliked people generally. I wasn't anxious to start playing the field as a super-salesman. It was remarkable enough to me how such a nomad rebel could be so comfortable around people.

Recalling Aquino, touring a casino in Reno while I watched, I was thoroughly amazed at his ready reserves of energy; his confident sportsmanship, able to play the game with any patron who preferred solitude and found incredulously that this ugly scab was lovable as Disney and versatile as clay.

Aquino's repulsive smile stretched across his face. It that face could launch ships, anyone's could. He probably could write a book called, "I'm Great, You're Great and Together We're Pretty Extraordinary." It was an exquisite character setting at my small dining table, except that my table had already become his table.

Rachel set next to me. "When do we get hitched?" I asked casually.

Rachel wrapped an arm around mine and placed her thin hand over mine, dark and calloused.

"Now that Joe is gone, must we be joined by another?"

"I would like it better," I persisted, realizing this was actually the first time I'd ever taken an independent position with them. Uncertain what Aquino thought, I decided I'd better not compromise on this one, if for no other reason than to establish Aquino's respect. I guessed to gain Aquino's respect meant Rachel's would not be far behind.

"I think it silly. We need no one outside of my family. You are my man."

"I rather be your husband."

"Papa will marry us. They can do that on boats."

"But, we're not at sea, so it doesn't matter." I smiled and caressed her hand as I felt her stiffen up slightly. I wasn't through, yet.

"I love you, Miss Rosen," I set up, facing her, boldly pronouncing my intentions in a fashion which seemed so out of character for me. I considered dropping to one knee as I wondered how she'd respond. Startled at the sound of her maiden name, I added, "I want to be joined to you, not only legally, but spiritually. I've lost you too many times before. I never want to lose you again. I know you may see it as frivolous – even foolish, but to me it's basic as breathing and eating. I'm not taking shortcuts with you. The courtship has begun. I've not won your heart until I see that wedding ring on your finger and heard you tell anyone who'll listen that you'll be my wife. In that way, it's official; it's final; it's formal."

She gazed at her bare ring finger as I offered a small peck, shamelessly luring to seal a pact – a covenant – to meld our differences – to secure the responsibilities of our commitment.

She accepted my offer with a ravenous, greedy kiss, locked securely against my mouth, warm as summer earth.

Fortunately, the aura carried us through. Rachel had no drivers license nor birth certificate to positively identify her. That forbad any civil service. Fortunately, Id met a pastor a couple years earlier after I'd last seen Aquino and Rachel. He remembered me, although I'd been selectively one of the passive members of the congregation, occupying seats near the back and involved in absolutely nothing. Despite the fact I'd quit attending, I was reminded of one lesson I'd taken from those months – that those of us who contributed little or nothing usually got little or nothing back. I related this to Rachel who barely understood. She'd never stepped inside a church. The misconceptions and superstitions she'd constructed around churches almost balked her acceptance of marriage.

She was unmistakably disappointed when she did go in. It was a small chapel with plain, white walls, regular windows, and a bare wooden podium up front. No grandeur. No more than a sanctified meeting hall. She'd expected something more – goddy.

The entire wedding took fifteen long and glorious minutes and we were wed. I was surprised ow scared I was – actually getting married for the first time. Michal attended with his family. They signed as witnesses, although I got the distinct feeling neither Michal nor his wife approved. I later overheard Michal telling Aquino, "He had his chance!" I presumed he was talking about me, but I wasn't sure. Rachel reminded me

Joe and Michal had always gotten along well, which was unusual for either of them.

The reception was a chat time around the dining table in my apartment. My humble home had never ventured such a feast. I had to laugh when Michal's wife had offered to prepare the food and Rachel argued and insisted she do it. She relented, accepting the weak argument that you don't cook on your wedding day. It was just another frivolous tradition to reject.

Eventually, I learned the actual reason she'd wanted to cook was because she'd never before used an oven. It was an exciting, new opportunity, more exciting than any other part of my small apartment and, in some ways, more compelling and adventuresome than our wedding.

I teased that at least once a month I dusted the oven whether it needed it or not. Rachel whapped me with a spatula while planting a hug-wrapped kiss upon me and whispering the couldn't wait to get me in bed tonight. Then, she reached down, giggled and chided, "Just making sure." It would've been more fun if the whole family hadn't been there, laughing and enjoying the show. Blushing, I realized it was probably akin to a family initiation. I hadn't married just Rachel, but her entire family which would make sleeping arrangements interesting. I joked to myself. I lit a cigarette and accepted a shot from Michal. Rachel squeezed in next to me.

"Thank you," she whispered, intimately seasoned.

"For what?" pulling my fingers down her long, black hair.

"For coming back for me – and for this wedding. Even if I think it foolish, I see it makes it right for you. And well, okay – it has also been fun."

"I love you," I reminded.

She smiled brightly and took a small bite of my ear. I returned her caress and playfully threatened to hold her down if she didn't behave herself. She stood her ground, assuring me she could take care of herself and daring me to try.

We playfully wrestled until I unexpectedly realized we were alone. The party had moved out to the motorhome and there was nothing to stop us from further discovering each other. Her demeanor also settled, ready to net me. I expected she didn't really consider us married before consummation, but this time we had a relationship already underway which would only add to the love we already shared.

As she approached in a distinctly notorious mating stance, I recalled the shy child who'd first approached me. Somehow it seemed natural to request, "Your tent or mine?" Smiling, I added, "I'll bring the candles. You bring the beans."

She shook her head in mock disgust and gave me a wonderful hug. I returned the embrace, welcoming therapy to revive the comatose soul. Yet, mostly I realized, before this moment, we could've parted company in bittersweet acceptance; survivors alone once again. Now we'd never be complete or whole to be separated again.

Our embrace included new life; lives unleashed. We'd finally discovered us - living for us; sharing after us; dancing with us; exactly like us.

An awful lot like us.

After The End

Just a quick note from the Author: I probably should have put this tidbit at the beginning of the novel, but I suspect most people don't care for Introductions or Forwards or whatever before you get to enjoy the actual story.

This first chapter is the first work of fiction I ever composed. Visiting a friend in Vallejo, CA right after I got out of the US Navy in 1977, he had to go back to work. He had an old typewriter and lots of yellow onion sheets, so I entertained myself by writing the first part of this story. I had no idea what would come forth until it flowed off my fingertips. I was thrilled with my first composition. I shared it with friends, learned the first lessons of editing and more.

Two years later, after I'd crafted a few more short stories, I revisited An Awful Lot Like Me, and decided it needed a sequel. So, the two years later literally is also two years later for the story and characters.

After that, I started writing novels, finishing my first work in 1981. Some thirteen years later, rummaging through a drawer looking for Navy papers, I found the two old stories. It was truly pleasing to see my early work. It was still a great story, but awfully written. It's actually a BIG blessing for an author to see how much one has advanced as a writer and artist. I didn't jump on the story at the time, but it coaxed me to finish the story, so thirteen years later is also thirteen years later for the characters and story.

I have no idea why I thought of it, but last year I found all three stories and decided to put them together as a sweet novella. It may not be my Magnum Opus, but it is definitely very close to my heart. I pray you are also greatly blessed by this, my first work as a writer.

Be blessed always, Dave

www.ingramcontent.com/pod-product-compliance
Lightning Source LLC
Chambersburg PA
CBHW022043170626
46808CB00003B/1342